SIX RIDERS . . .
COMING AT A GALLOP

Lighthorse stopped and twisted in his saddle with his right hand on the horse's rump, and watched them. Then he looked at his partner and the woman.

"Oh, boy," he said. "They found us."

Sammy said, "I don't know where we're running to, but let's ride. Mrs. Wilcox, it's time to whip your pony into a run!"

They got their animals into a lope. The mule would trot all day; but it wasn't used to running with a load on its back, and it pulled on the lead rope. The woman's sorrel horse was running well, and she was leaning over the saddle horn, her dark hair streaming, her divided skirt whipping high on her legs.

Looking back, Sammy could see the outlaws gaining. He yelled at Lighthorse, "We're gonna have to make a stand somewhere."

"I'm looking for a place!"

They rode, trying to urge the pack animals to run faster. The riders behind them were closer. Soon they would be in rifle range.

There was only one way this could end. . . .

MOUNTAIN MARAUDERS

DOYLE TRENT

ZEBRA BOOKS
KENSINGTON PUBLISHING CORP.

For Joyce, my wife, my partner, my best friend.

One

The sound of gunshots came from far away, carried on a cool breeze that swept over the high cedar ridges of the Pinos Altos Range. The two young men reined their horses to a stop and listened.

"About a mile and a half, I'd say."

"Maybe a little farther."

Faint popping sounds continued. The light-skinned, sandy-haired young man allowed, "That ain't somebody hunting meat."

"No," the dark-complexioned one said. "That's somebody trying to kill somebody."

"Could be a detail from Bayard shooting it out with some of Victorio's braves."

Nodding, the dark one said, "Could be. But it's not a big battle. Not enough shooting."

They sat their saddles quietly for a moment. Both carried six-guns, butts forward in military flap holsters on their left sides, and lever-action rifles in boots under their right legs.

"Well," the light-skinned one said finally, "it's none of our business."

"No. Unless . . ."

"Unless what?"

"Unless it's some Chiricahuas killing a couple of white men."

"If we ride down there, they'll turn their guns on us."

"That's so." The dark one mulled that over. "But suppose the white eyes are putting up a fight, and suppose we come at the Apaches from behind."

"If there ain't too many of 'em, that might discourage 'em."

"They're still shooting. They ain't killed all the white eyes yet."

"I thought I was through fighting Apaches."

"Me, too. But what if . . ."

"You still hate 'em, don't you, the Chiricahuas and Jicarillas?"

"Not as much as I used to, but what if they're killing some of your white brothers."

"Well hell, let's go see what's what."

They turned their horses downhill where there was no trail. The horses were bays, the difference being a white hind pastern and a snipe nose on one, while the other's legs were black from the knees and hocks down. The dark-skinned young man led a gray mule carrying a light load. The hill was steep enough that they had to traverse it to get to the bottom. There they pushed through oak brush to a shallow ravine, followed it a quarter mile, then climbed out of it and rode through more scrub oaks, over broken shale and into a scattering of cedars.

"It can't be much farther," the fair-skinned one said. "I don't hear any gunfire, though. Maybe we're too late."

His companion only grunted. Then two more shots came from directly ahead of them. "Down under this hill." The dark one pulled his rifle free. "We keep going straight ahead and we'll come up on 'em."

They rode at a walk, eyes taking in everything. When they came over the crest of a cedar hill to where they could see down into a narrow ravine they reined up again, surprised at what they saw.

"They ain't Indians."

"Nope. White men. Shooting at white men."

"Looks like a woman down there." The light-skinned one squinted, pulled his wide hat brim down to shade his eyes. "It is, wearing a dress. Sure as hell. A man's with her."

"Yup, and them four jacklegs are trying to shoot 'em out of that gulch."

"Whose side are we on, Lighthorse?"

"On the side of the dress. She's no gunfighter."

"Well, she's the one who needs help." The fair-skinned one lifted his rifle, dismounted and handed the reins to his partner. He put the rifle to his shoulder and fired. The horses snorted at the sudden explosion and rolled their eyes.

Two of the four men down there were circling to the south, trying to get into a position to shoot up the gulch. The other two were snapping shots into the side of the gulch opposite them, keeping the man and woman from rising up and shooting back.

At the sound of the rifle shot from the top of the hill, all four stopped dead still, their heads swiveling to see where the shot had come from. The young man fired another round into the ground near the feet of the two who had been circling south. They jumped back.

From the hill, the two young men could see the surprised expressions on the faces of the four. Then they were being shot at.

Lighthorse said, "I'll get these animals back out of sight; then I'll help you." He led the two horses and the mule back over the crest of the hill. The fair-skinned young man knelt on one knee and put a bullet into the ground near the feet of the nearest man below him. A brief volley came his way, spanging off the rocks, knocking leaves off the scrub oaks. He levered and fired again.

Then his partner was back, firing two quick shots into the ground in front of the four. "We trying to hit anybody?" he asked.

"Not yet. We don't know who we're shooting at."

The dark-skinned one pulled his head down instinctively when a rifle slug sang a deadly song past his right ear. "Well, they're trying to hit us."

"Let's send a volley near their feet and heads and see what happens."

They fired, levered, fired, levered, fired. The four men downhill backed up. More rifle slugs were sent their way. Then they turned and ran, bullets smacking into the rocky ground near their feet.

"I see their horses. Back in the yellow pines."

"White man no like odds now. Give 'em up."

Grinning at his partner, the other said, "It's your Muache shooting that's got 'em scared."

Patting the stock of his rifle, the one called Lighthorse said, "White man make 'em good gun. Shoot fast."

Still grinning, his partner said, "You'd better not talk like that when we get down there. They'll think old Cochise has come back to haunt 'em."

"Cochise spirit still around. Kill 'em white eyes."

"Yeah, and the spirit's name is Victorio."

"I'll get 'em horses."

"Get *the* horses, you danged blanket ass."

The dark face split into a good-natured grin, white teeth gleaming. "You better not call the Apaches blanket ass."

"I ain't gonna get within hollering distance of another damned Apache."

They rode downhill, slowly, eyes on the yellow pines ahead, rifles in their hands. "I do believe those four are gone, but we can't be sure."

"They could come up again on our left flank. They can see now that there's only two of us."

"Yeah, and we're out in open terrain."

"We need to get down there in that defiladed area. Wonder if that man and woman are friendly."

With a snort, the light-skinned one chided, "Defiladed area. That's a gulch, ravine, arroyo. We ain't in the damned army now."

"Holler at 'em, Sammy, and see what happens."

The fair-skinned one reined up and yelled, "Hey. Who's down there?" When he got no answer, he yelled again. "Hey down there, we're friends. Amigos. Are you still alive?"

Finally a face appeared over the top of the gulch, a woman's face, a white woman, scared. The end of a rifle barrel appeared beside the face, but it was pointed skyward.

She yelled, "What . . . who are you?"

"We're not your enemy. We mean you no harm. Can we come closer without getting shot?"

A hank of dark hair curled over her forehead from

under a wide-brim hat. "Who are you?" Her voice was still scared.

"We're headed for Pinos Altos. We heard the gunfire. We're coming over."

They rode forward slowly, rifles across their saddles now. When they were close enough to see into the gulch, they saw a man on his back, eyes squinched, teeth clenched. His gray shirt was bloody.

"Is he hurt bad?" Sammy asked.

"He's badly wounded," the woman said. "He . . . he shot back as long as he could."

"We're coming down."

They had to go south a hundred feet to find a bank that their horses and pack mule could slide down without losing their footing. Sammy dismounted and knelt beside the downed man. He was middle-aged, with a short, trimmed beard and brown hair streaked with gray. He wore baggy wool pants and jack boots. His shapeless black hat lay near his head.

"Sir," Sammy said, "we're friends. We just happened along. I'm a former medical orderly with the United States cavalry. Mind if I take a look?"

The squinched eyes opened, studied Sammy's face, then turned toward the dark-skinned one. Alarm flared for a second.

"He's a Muache Ute," Sammy said. "He's on our side."

The eyes closed again, squinched in pain.

Sammy unbuttoned the man's shirt. The bullet hole was a few inches above the hip bone, just under the bottom rib. Looking around, Sammy spotted two saddle horses and a packhorse standing reins down fifty feet up the gulch. "Do you have anything to make a bandage out of, ma'am? Any medicine at all?"

"N-no." She knelt beside the man's head and stroked his hair. "How . . . bad is it?"

Shaking his head sadly, Sammy said, "I won't try to fool you, ma'am. It's bad. Probably punctured the kidney. He needs a surgeon."

Voice shaky, she asked, "Where . . . is the nearest hospital?"

"Fort Bayard, ma'am. Between here and Silver City. Lighthorse and I, we're known there." Sammy glanced up at his partner, who had climbed to the top of the gulch, rifle ready, eyes searching. Looking back at the woman, Sammy said, "What I don't know is how to get this gentleman there."

"We—I have to do something. I can't just let him die."

Sammy considered that and asked, "Is he your husband?"

"Yes."

"Do you have a handkerchief, or anything?"

She pulled a small, dainty handkerchief from the one pocket on her dress. He pressed it tightly to the bullet hole for a full minute, then lifted it and saw that it had slowed the bleeding somewhat but had not stopped it. "Sir," Sammy said to the man, "can you stand up?"

The eyes, pain-filled, opened. "I'll try."

"Let me give you a hand." With Sammy's help, the man got to his feet, but his legs were trying to collapse from under him. "I can see," Sammy said, "that you're in no condition to get on a horse. We'll carry you."

Looking up at his partner, Sammy yelled, "Hey, Lighthorse, any sign of anybody?"

Lighthorse looked back. "Naw. I think they've pulled their freight out of here."

"Come down here and give me a hand."

While the Indian slid down into the ravine, Sammy lowered the injured man onto his back again. "We're gonna have to carry him, Lighthorse. We can rig a stretcher out of a couple of those yellow pine trunks and the tarp on our pack."

"I'll go cut down a couple of young trees." The Indian went to the gray mule and pulled an axe out of one of the canvas panniers. The woman held her husband's head in her lap and stroked his hair.

"I reckon," Lighthorse said, dropping two long, slim tree trunks onto the ground, "we can tie the ends of these poles to the stirrups on two horses and carry him between the horses."

"We can try. If that doesn't work, we'll have to carry him by hand."

"We going to Bayard?"

"That's the closest place I know of where this man can get medical help." Turning to the woman, Sammy said, "Fort Bayard is, I'd guess, about twelve miles southeast. There's a mining camp called Buckhorn fourteen-sixteen miles southwest, but I doubt there's a surgeon there. Would you happen to know whether there is?"

"I—no. I'm afraid there isn't."

"It's got to be Bayard, then."

Glancing at the western horizon, Lighthorse said, "Be dark in a couple of hours. Let's see how far we can get."

It took a while to wrap the canvas tarp around the two slim tree trunks and tie it in place with a lash rope from the pack mule. The two young men carried it back to the downed man and the woman. The woman was sitting on her feet with her husband's head in her lap. Tears were streaming down her face.

Between sobs she said, "He . . . his eyes opened and he won't talk to me. I . . . I'm afraid . . ."

Quickly, Sammy knelt, felt for a pulse in the man's wrist, then the throat. He leaned over and put his ear to the man's chest. Straightening, he shook his head sadly. "I'm sorry, ma'am. I'm sure sorry."

Two

All they could do was walk away a short distance and let the woman cry. Now and then they heard a sob, but mostly she cried quietly. Lighthorse kicked the stretcher they'd made and grumbled, "We won't need that."

"No. I knew he wouldn't last through the night, but for her sake I thought we ought to at least try to get him to a surgeon."

"Wonder what those jacklegs wanted? What were they after?"

Nodding at the packhorse, Sammy said, "You can guess."

"Something valuable, and it ain't United States government greenbacks."

"Nope. If it takes a horse to carry it, it has to be gold."

"Yep. That horse is packing gold, sure as hell."

"And you can guess why they were traveling cross-country instead of following a road."

"Road agents. I've heard there's more robbers and killers in these parts than honest people."

"I've heard the same. If they think somebody might

have something worth stealing, they'll get it. Nobody carries anything valuable on a stagecoach nowadays."

"That's so. Well, what are we gonna do about her—and him?"

With a shrug, Sammy said, "I reckon that's up to her. I'll ask her. After she's had her cry."

It was a solemn procession that rode out of the ravine at sundown: two men and a woman on horseback, leading two pack animals and a saddle horse with the tarp-covered body of a man tied facedown across the saddle. Lighthorse promised a three-quarter moon, and he was sure he could find Fort Bayard in the moonlight.

Looking at the western horizon, at the sky, the Indian took the lead, heading southeast. They rode through a stand of yellow pines, crossed another dry ravine and pushed through an acre of green buck brush. By the time they topped another cedar-studded ridge the sun had dropped out of sight, but the moon hadn't appeared yet. Lighthorse was leading the party by instinct.

They rode quietly. Sammy decided it was best to let the woman talk when she felt like it or keep quiet if she felt like it. Once they reached open country, she rode up beside him. "Did I hear you say your friend is a Ute Indian?"

"Yes, ma'am. He's been a scout for the Sixth Cavalry for a long time."

"The Utes are friendly, then?"

"We haven't had any trouble with them. They, uh, the Utes and the Jicarilla Apaches aren't the best of friends." He pronounced Jicarilla as "Hicariya."

"I see. Except for the color of his skin and hair he looks like a white man."

"Like I said, he's lived with us for a long time. He's learned to read and write English. As a matter of fact, he can read and write better than most white folks in this territory."

"You were in the army?"

"Yes, ma'am. We mustered out a couple of weeks ago, out of Fort Union, up north."

"I see." Her voice held a touch of grief, but the expression on her face was hidden in the dark. "Well, I'm certainly lucky that you came along. Those men, they wanted to rob us."

"We figured that." He didn't ask why, deciding to let her tell about it if she wanted to.

She fell silent again, dropping back to the end of the procession, leading her packhorse. Sammy led the horse carrying the dead man, and Lighthorse led the gray mule. Their mounts carried them uphill and downhill, through timber and elder brush. Finally, Sammy said, "It's darker than a stack of black cats. Where's that moon you promised, Lighthorse?"

"It'll show up over east in another ten minutes."

"You sure we're headed in the right direction?"

"I know where we are, don't you?"

"Well, I could get disoriented in the dark."

"We've been over this country before."

"Yeah, but . . . I'll admit it, I don't have your instincts."

As promised, the three-quarter moon came up over a rocky ridge, and Sammy knew then that they were going in the right direction and would get to Fort Bayard in another hour.

In the moonlight, the fort looked deserted, but the two young men knew the clapboard barracks and the adobe office buildings were still occupied by the twelfth regiment of the Sixth Cavalry. Guards were posted behind the rock parapets, and the travelers had been spotted. When they came within yelling distance, they stopped.

"Hey," Sammy yelled, "we're ex-soldiers. My name is Samual Collins, the former Corporal Collins. Lighthorse Jones is with me."

A man's voice came back. "Lighthorse? Is that you out there?"

"Yeah, white man. I came back to see if you fellers are as ugly as you were the last time I saw you."

A chuckle, then, "Well, come on in, big chief redass."

"We've got a woman with us, and a dead man."

"Oh, excuse me, lady. I'll fetch the corporal of the guard, but you all can come on in."

All the post surgeon could do was dress the body in a clean shirt, which the woman produced from their packs, and lay it out straight on its back with the hands crossed over the stomach. A blacksmith chiseled the name on a flat slab of shale, and two troopers sawed and nailed pine boards for a plain coffin. Most of the regiment was on patrol, trying to protect the white settlers and the mining camps in the territory from marauding Apaches, so only a handful of troopers and two officers' wives attended the funeral. The post chaplain did the best he could without knowing anything about the deceased.

Burial was in a small cemetery under a brush-covered hill just outside the post. Most of the deceased were black troopers who had served with an all-black regiment of the Ninth Cavalry, but they were buried in a separate section.

When it was over the small group walked away, leaving behind a fresh grave and a two-foot-high tombstone with the message: Henry Wilcox, 1829-1875. The chaplain, a smallish man who always looked like he was about to choke on his white collar, walked beside the widow. She wore a long dark dress decorated with lace down the front and around the throat, a dress that had been loaned to her by one of the officers' wives. As she walked, she dabbed at her eyes and nose with a dainty lace handkerchief.

The former Corporal Collins and the former scout Lighthorse Jones bought a new canvas tarp at the sutler's store and started to lead their horses and mule outside the fort.

"Say," said a red-faced sergeant in a campaign hat, "I heered you two was gonna find a gulch of gold, or somethin'."

"Well," Lighthorse said, "you know how these outhouse rumors go."

"Where are you goin', if it's any of my business."

"When we decide, maybe we'll let you know. And maybe we won't."

"Haw. Bet you're gonna look for the mountain of gold that crazy German blabbed about."

"The rocks he had in his haversack weren't sandstones."

"No, but—haw, haw—he was so crazy he didn't know where he found 'em, and all he got for his troubles was a fancy coffin."

"Yeah, yeah." Lighthorse grinned. "Rave on cat shit, somebody'll cover you up."

"Haw, haw. You fellers, you danged civilians, don't have to sleep out there with the rattlesnakes and 'Paches. Roll out your beds over by the stables. Give your animals a good feed and a rest. Then go out in the mornin' and get your scalps lifted."

The two partners looked at each other; then Lighthorse said, "What do you think, Sammy? Wanta take him up on that?"

"Why not,"—Sammy grinned—"maybe we'll finally get something free from the army."

They no more than picked out a spot for their beds than a trooper who looked to be in his teens brought them a message. "That woman, that Missus Wilcox, ast me to tell you she wants to see you. She's over at the sutler's."

Message delivered, the trooper turned and headed for the barracks. The two partners looked at each other again. "I'd just as soon not have to listen to any thank-yous," Sammy said, "but I reckon it would be bad manners to ignore her."

"You go over without me. Tell her . . . oh, hell, I'll go with you."

She was waiting in front of the store, standing with her feet together and her hands clasped in front of her. She had changed from the dark dress to a long gray skirt and a blue cotton shirtwaist. "Is there someplace where we can talk without being overheard?" Sammy noticed then that she was sort of pretty, with her dark hair, gray eyes, shapely mouth and chin. She had to be younger than her husband.

"An army post is the last place you can find any privacy," Sammy said, "but . . ." He looked around, shook his head, then had an idea. "Maybe, if you wouldn't mind, we could go back to the cemetery. That's the only private place I know of."

"Very well."

The three of them walked to the cemetery, the woman between the two men. Near the fresh grave, she stopped and faced them. "I, uh, what I wanted to talk about is . . . well, you've probably guessed by now that we, my husband and I, were carrying something valuable."

"Yes, ma'am."

"I think I can trust you now. I mean, if you wanted to rob me, you had plenty of opportunities. What we're carrying is gold. My husband panned it over four years, and we have quite a lot of it. We were trying to get to Albuquerque where we believe there is a bank. From there we were going to go back to St. Louis."

"Uh-huh. And you couldn't travel the roads because of the road agents."

"We left town in the dark of night, hoping no one would know, but . . . you saw what happened."

"Yeah. I mean, yes, ma'am."

" 'Yeah' is good enough."

"What are you gonna do now?"

"Well, I was thinking, if you two gentlemen are footloose, if you have nothing else to do, I could hire you to accompany me to Albuquerque."

"Oh." Sammy frowned at that. Glancing at his partner, he saw Lighthorse was frowning, too. "Well, uh . . ."

"I'll pay you a hundred and fifty dollars each."

"What do you think, Lighthorse? How far is it to Albuquerque?"

"Over the mountains? Five-six days."

"If you gentlemen want to talk it over privately, I'll leave you alone for a while." She turned to walk away, then stopped. "I'll pay you two hundred dollars each." Then she walked to the edge of the cemetery.

"What do I think?" Lighthorse said. "I'll tell you what I think. Them four jacklegs will know by tomorrow night at the latest that her husband is dead, and they'll know she left with only the two of us for armed escorts. They'll be on our trail, and if they don't think four shooters are enough, they'll get some help."

"You're right. We'll damned sure earn that two hundred bucks."

"So what do you say?"

"That crazy German's diggings ain't gonna be found for a long time and maybe never. We've been shot at before, and you're damned hard to sneak up on."

"The sooner we get started the better."

"I'll tell her. I'll see you down at the stables."

Three

They rode out of the fort at sunup, three of them, leading two pack animals. The Indian took the lead, and his partner brought up the rear. They rode silently, each with his own thoughts. Sammy was wishing he hadn't gotten into this, but knowing he could find no excuse for refusing the woman. Except to say it was too dangerous. He was thinking it, but he wouldn't say it.

The woman was in mourning, wishing she could have buried her husband in St. Louis instead of in a tiny cemetery at a desolate army post in New Mexico Territory. She was wishing they'd never left St. Louis. So Henry Wilcox had failed in business. So he just had to come west and try to find his fortune. So, after four years of panning, digging and working that silly-looking sluice box, he had two one-pound leather bags of gold dust. Then finally, after living in near poverty, he found what he was looking for, what he believed was a rich vein. Now he was dead. All that work and hard living for nothing. Buried among the soldiers and Negroes, where none of his relatives would ever see the grave. Where she would never see it again.

So she now had wealth. Not a lot of wealth, but enough. That is if she could get these pack boxes of gold dust and nuggets to a bank or someplace where she could convert them to cash. That was a big if. She could be killed the same way Henry was killed, and the gold would end up in the hands of robbers and murderers.

Biting her lower lip to hold back the tears, she said under her breath, "Why didn't I try harder, Henry, to talk you out of leaving home?"

Lighthorse Jones was wondering whether he'd done the smart thing by mustering out of the army. He'd had a home there. Fort Union was a good place, like a small town, with stores, a school, a church, even a theater and a regimental band. He was treated as an equal there, and he'd learned to speak, read and write the white man's language. The future for an Indian was with the white men. Even old Cochise knew that.

The old chief had fought the white and Mexican soldiers in four states and two countries. He'd fought more battles and led more raids than he could count. But, the way it was told, the old war-horse's last words of advice to his people were to forever live in peace with the whites.

Living in peace wouldn't be easy for Lighthorse. The Apaches hated him because he'd scouted for their enemy, and too many of the whites hated him because he . . . well, because he was an Indian.

Both Indians and whites had their reasons for hatred. One side was as guilty as the other. That was why Lighthorse had mustered out of the army. He blamed both sides and he sympathized with both sides. He had every reason to hate the Apache and he owed the army. But he hoped he would be allowed to be neutral.

They were in a country of low hills studded with cedar and piñon. A flat-topped butte jutted up on the west, its top protected from erosion by a shale cap. To the east, the highest peaks of the Black Range loomed dark and mysterious. Both men had been in the Black Range of mountains. They'd fought the Apache there, buried their victims. It was beautiful country. Wild and beautiful. But as long as Victorio and his Chiricahuas were raiding and killing, it was also dangerous.

When the sun was straight overhead, they stopped to eat army hardtack while the horses grazed on the sideoats, grama and crested wheatgrass. Meager meal over, the two men walked behind a boulder and emptied their bladders.

"Ever camp with a woman before?" Sammy asked.

"Yeah. Indians."

"Sure. Of course. What did you use for toilets?"

"Make 'em guess, white eyes."

Chuckling, Sammy said, "Naw, I think I'll drop the subject."

The pack animals, carrying dead weight, would get no rest until they were unloaded, so the procession soon mounted and rode on. At sundown, they stopped and off-saddled beside a trickle of a stream that came down from the Black Range.

Sammy said, "We figure we'll be safe out in the open tonight, Mrs. Wilcox. If anybody is following us, it will take them a day, probably, to get organized and started. We'd better let the horses graze in the open while we can."

"Then you're convinced we will be followed?" She stood wearily beside her horse, leaning against its shoulder. Her broad-brim hat wasn't a man's hat after all, Sammy decided. It was the same except for a wide band of red ribbon and a bow knot. Her long gray skirt was divided so she could straddle a horse.

"It's more than likely, ma'am."

"You don't have to be so formal, now that we're traveling partners. Call me Mrs. Wilcox, or better yet, Regina." She smiled a weak smile. It was the first time he'd seen her smile.

She was a handsome woman.

Back from staking out the horses, Lighthorse said, "We heard plenty of gunfire before we came up on you back there in that ravine. I hope you were doing some of the shooting."

"Oh, yes. My husband bought me a Winchester repeating rifle and taught me how to shoot. I'd much rather not have to."

Grinning, white teeth gleaming against the dark face, Lighthorse commented, "Me, too."

Supper was fresh elk steak broiled over an open fire, with more hardtack, canned peaches and coffee. Sammy said, "Fresh meat won't keep long in a pack pannier, but it sure is good while it lasts. It'll be side meat from here on." They rolled out their tarp-covered beds on the grass near the creek, the woman on one side of the creek and the men on the other.

Whispering, Sammy said, "How much gold do you reckon she's got?"

"About fifty pounds in each one of them two pack boxes."

"If we can get her to the big city, she won't have to worry about living expenses for a long time."

"Yeah, if."

Breakfast was fried bacon, coffee and hardtack. While Sammy washed the skillet and tin plates in the creek,

Lighthorse loaded the pack animals. He tied the pack boxes on the brown horse with a box hitch, and the load on the gray mule with a diamond hitch. The woman saddled her own horse.

Staying west of the Black Canyon and Granite Peak, they crossed a high prairie covered with brown grass, blue sagebrush and green yucca, then rode into the Diablo Range where they stopped for a noon rest.

While the woman and Sammy ate cold fried bacon, dried apples and more of the hardtack, Lighthorse walked back to a high point, stood next to a stunted, twisted pine tree and studied their back trail. Rejoining them, he allowed, "They ain't got as far as the prairie yet." He tore into a slab of bacon with his strong white teeth and chewed rapidly.

"They could still be less than a day behind us," Sammy said. "But they'll try their durndest to catch up, even if they kill their horses doing it."

"We're moving right along; but the pack animals can't make good time packing dead weight, and we don't want to take a chance on getting a horse hurt."

"Perhaps," the woman said, "there's no one following us."

"That could be so," Sammy said, "but we have to proceed with the utmost caution." Then, realizing he was talking like a soldier, he said, "I mean we have to be ready. We can't be sure of anything."

That evening they were sure.

Lighthorse's jaw was set when he walked back to their camp under some jack pines. "They're back there and still coming. While we're resting, they're traveling."

"How many?"

"Don't know. I got a couple of glimpses, is all."

"They won't ride all night. Their horses are no tougher than ours."

"They ain't worried about saving their horses. They're thinking if they run theirs down, they can take ours."

"Well, our horses ought to get their fill on this grass tonight and a rest. If it comes to a horse race, we'll be better mounted."

"The pack animals will slow us down, but maybe we'll have a chance to find a place to fort up."

Mrs. Wilcox had spoken little all day, but now, with a slight tremor in her voice, she said, "We're going to be shot at again. By robbers and murderers."

"Maybe not, Mrs. Wilcox. Maybe they won't catch us."

"We'll keep up a steady trot when we get down on the plains," Lighthorse said. "We'll be riding again at first light."

Breakfast could wait. Munching cold, stale hardtack, they were five miles closer to Albuquerque by sunup. They crossed West Fork Creek at mid-morning, then the Middle Fork. There, on the far bank, they stopped and let the horses graze while they divided two cans of beans and some dried fruit. Then they were in the Elk Mountains, with high rocky ridges, green pine-covered hills and deep canyons. They rode at a trot where the ground wasn't uphill, but most of the terrain was uphill.

A big turkey gobbler walked out of some elder brush, turned and walked back in, out of their sight. "You're in no danger," Sammy said to the bird. "We're not hunting meat." In a small grassy park four deer, two of them bucks with wide racks, threw their heads up, watched them a moment, then bounded into the timber.

"Ever seen a grizzly, Lighthorse?"

"I seen 'em and ran from 'em. Them brutes can run as fast as a horse for a hundred feet or so. And durned near as big. And mean as a rattlesnake."

"I hear the Indians put a high value on a grizzly hide."

"Silvertip hides make pretty robes. Mighty pretty in the winter. Not so pretty in the summer."

They rode through timber, an acre of willows, then up a rocky ridge. The ridge was steep enough that they had to stop twice and let their horses blow before getting to the top.

Over the top and down into a narrow, grassy valley, they came to a trickle of a stream. They got down and drank. The two men lay on their bellies, faces in the water. The woman dipped a tin cup into the water. "It's running northwest," Sammy said. "We're across the divide now."

"We'll be out of these hills by dark."

Shortly before dark they could see down onto the Plains of San Agustin. Lighthorse reined up. "Let's find us a defiladed area—excuse me, Mr. Civilian—an arroyo where we can fort up. I'd rather fight it out with 'em up here than down there in open country."

"Now you're thinking like a soldier."

It was almost dark before they came to a narrow arroyo deep enough to hide the horses in. But after offsaddling, the men led the animals out of the arroyo to a grassy spot and hobbled them.

"Them jacklegs won't catch up with us 'til after midnight," Lighthorse said. "Best let these animals graze awhile, keep 'em strong."

"Maybe they won't catch up tonight."

"They will. Their horses will be on their last legs, but they'll catch up."

"I'll take the first watch."

"I'll stay up, too, 'til it's time to bring the animals down where they won't get shot. If we lose even one horse, we'll have to leave our stuff behind."

"Well," Sammy said, "we've been shot at before. I just hope there ain't too many of 'em."

Four

Smoke wouldn't be seen in the dark, and the campers believed their pursuers weren't close enough to see a small fire. So they fried cured side meat, made coffee and opened a can of beans. After they ate, they stomped out the fire, and Sammy climbed to the top of the arroyo and sat in the grass near the grazing horses, a rifle across his lap.

Lighthorse and the woman sat in the dark, silently, until she said, "Excuse me for saying so, but you don't look like the Indians I've seen."

With a dry chuckle, Lighthorse said, "Most white folks recognize me as an Indian almost as far away as they can see me."

"I didn't mean . . . yes, you have the skin color; but you dress like a white man, and your hair is cut the same as a white man, and you speak English very well."

"I've lived with white soldiers a long time now."

"I'm sorry if I was too forward. You seem to be a very nice person."

"I'm not offended."

They were silent again, but she couldn't help sneaking glances at him. He was handsome, tall and straight, with high cheekbones, a straight, aristocratic nose, wide mouth and strong chin. Dark eyes. Women back east would consider him one of the most handsome men they'd ever seen. Mrs. Wilcox, however, was still mourning her dead husband, and there wasn't a man in the world who would interest her. Finally, she said, "Good night, Mr., uh, Lighthorse."

"Good night, Mrs. Wilcox."

Yes, Lighthorse thought, sitting alone in the dark, I've lived with the white soldiers a long time. He'd considered, only a short while ago, going back to live with his relatives on the Ute reservation near the Colorado border. Lighthorse and Sammy had mustered out together and traveled to Santa Fe, where they'd split up. But Lighthorse had promised he'd be back in a week. Sammy had said he'd stick around.

He almost wished he hadn't gone to the reservation. The Utes, once proud hunters and warriors, were living in near squalor, depending on the white agent of the U.S. government for their living. With no buffalo, they had to make their tepees from deer skins, and deer were not plentiful on the reservation. Most of the Indians lived in shacks made of rough sawn wood covered with tar paper. A few shacks were made of rocks.

Lighthorse knew his mother and father were dead, but the last time he'd visited the Muache Ute camp both his grandparents had still been alive.

Now he found his old grandmother, with a thousand wrinkles in her round face and no teeth at all, living alone in a one-room shack. Wearing a plain brown dress issued by the government agent. In spite of eyes sunken deeply in her brown skin, she recognized him immediately.

Speaking in the Ute language, she said, "My son. It

is good to see you. You are tall and strong. The white man has treated you well."

"Yes, Grandmother. I am well fed, and I have learned the white man's ways."

Without getting up from the narrow spring bed, she studied his face. "It is wise to learn the white man's ways. The old way of life is gone forever."

They talked of the old life, the years when the buffalo abounded on the plains, and the deer and elk were plentiful in the mountains. They talked of Lighthorse's mother and father who had died of smallpox, a disease that had wiped out almost half the tribe, a disease brought by the white man. At supper time, the old woman got up and built a fire in the government issue sheet metal combination heating and cooking stove. They ate stew made of a small amount of beef and potatoes and carrots, weakened by too much water to make the food go further.

Soon after the dishes were washed, the old woman said she was tired and had to go to bed. Lighthorse unrolled his bed on the floor.

He spent another day and night on the reservation, visiting with old friends. They, too, talked about the old days. Some were bitter. They had fought the white man, but there were too many soldiers. Many braves had died. They had no choice now but to live on the reservation.

Would they fight again if they had a chance?

"No," said an old man, bent and wrinkled. "The fighting spirit is gone from the young people. Now we are wards of the U.S. government. We are like animals."

When he said goodbye to his grandmother, tears were welling up in his eyes. But an Indian didn't cry. And an Indian didn't kiss and hug.

"Goodbye, my grandmother. May the good spirits be with you."

"Goodbye, my son. Be brave. Be honest. Never forget the pride and honor of your ancestors."

"I will never forget, and I will always keep my pride and honor."

Riding back to Santa Fe, he'd been saddened by the way his people were living. But while they had talked of the old days, they had avoided mentioning the hard times, the famines when the winters were long and cruel and the game was scarce. When the children's stomachs were swollen from hunger. They hadn't talked about the diseases that had killed many people before the white man came along. And they hadn't talked about the many young braves who had died in the wars with the Jicarillas and the Cheyennes, about how they'd had to live in constant fear of being attacked by their neighbors. They had complained of no longer having the freedom to go where they pleased, but they hadn't mentioned the danger of wandering onto another tribe's hunting grounds.

Yet, Lighthorse knew that if it were possible to go back to the old life, he'd go.

Tonight he stood and climbed out of the arroyo, gripping his rifle. He whispered in the dark, "It's me, Lighthorse. I'll help with the animals."

"Here. I'm over here."

"Do your ears tell you anything?"

"They haven't said a word. Neither have my eyes. I was sure a full moon followed a three-quarter moon."

"Sometimes no moon follows a three-quarter moon. But not tonight. It's coming. Probably just in time to light the way for those jacklegs."

"Then we'd better get these horses down in that gulch where they won't be seen."

"Or shot."

Working by feel and dim starlight, they located the animals, untied the hobbles and led them down into the deepest part of the arroyo. The sound of hoofbeats and horses blowing through their nostrils awakened the woman.

"Is there danger?"

"Not yet, ma'am, Mrs. Wilcox."

To Sammy, Lighthorse said, "You go ahead and get some shut-eye. I'll keep watch for a couple of hours."

With a tarp under him and folded back over him, Sammy slept. He'd been in battle before, and he'd learned, like any good soldier, to take his sleep when he had a chance. He slept for more than two hours. It was his partner's shaking him and whispering that awakened him.

"Huh?" He sat up immediately.

"Shh. They're here."

"Uh-oh." Quickly, Sammy pulled on his boots, stood and picked up his rifle. "How many?"

"Don't know. Can't see 'em all. But at least five."

They climbed to the top edge of the arroyo, to where they could see over the top. A full moon had showed itself now, and while the treetops were visible, the ground under the trees was in shadow. "See 'em," Lighthorse whispered.

"I see one. Two. They don't know we're here, but they're being cautious."

"They see this gulch, and they think we might be in here."

"Be daylight soon. Then they'll know for sure."

"I see the same two you see. What say we pick 'em off."

"Yeah. Don't say, 'Halt, who goes there,' or anything. We know they intend to kill us."

"I'll take the one on the right; you take the one on the left. We'll try to fire at the same time."

"Gotcha."

Carefully, silently, both men pulled their rifle levers down to half cock, felt with their fingers to be certain there were bullets in the chambers, then pulled the hammers back to full cock. When their targets rode out of the shadows, they lined up the sights.

"Ready?"

"Yeah."

Lighthorse fired first, and Sammy's rifle cracked a split second later. The explosions rent the quiet of the night like a thunderbolt.

Two men fell from their horses. The horses spun away from their fallen riders and trotted back the way they'd come.

"Move," Sammy said.

"I'm moving."

Gunfire came from behind the trees and rocks. Bullets kicked up dirt near where the two partners had been. More rifle slugs whined over the arroyo and ricocheted with a scream off the rocks.

Sammy fired at a muzzle flash, then ducked and moved four feet to his left. A shot cracked from Lighthorse's rifle.

A stifled scream came from the woman, and Sammy yelled, "Stay down, stay down."

Then the shooting stopped. The night was silent again.

Minutes passed. Lighthorse whispered, "You still over there, Sammy?"

"I'm here. Think they're waiting for daylight?"

"Maybe. Maybe not. They might be trying to out-Indian an Indian and sneak around behind us."

"I'll go over to the other side."

"The two we shot are still lying there."

"I don't know how many there are, but there's two less."

"If you need any help over there, holler."

"You can bet I will. Mrs. Wilcox, how are you?"

"I-I'm all right. I've got my rifle ready."

"Good. But don't expose yourself yet. Not yet."

Trying to move without sound, Sammy climbed down into the arroyo and halfway up the other side. He picked a position where only his hat and face showed above the arroyo.

Resting on his left side, boots digging into the dirt for a foothold, Sammy let his eyes rove over the ground in front of him. They were in a fairly good spot, but were it not for the stunted pines and cedars around them, it would have been a lot better. The field of fire was not clear by any means. But then they'd had no choice.

It was ironic, he thought, how the white soldiers, the ones who Lighthorse considered friends, joked and kidded him about his dark skin. But when it came to night guarding they all wished they could darken their skin. My face must be shining in this moonlight like a bull's-eye lantern, Sammy thought.

With nothing happening, Sammy turned his head to see what Mrs. Wilcox was doing. That motion saved his life. The bullet came from the shadow of a tree and buzzed past his ear like an angry hornet. He'd been seen. Time to move. Scrambling, boots trying to find footholds, he moved six feet to his left and raised his head above the top of the arroyo again.

He saw a shadow detach itself from a short cedar, and he raised up enough to aim and fire.

More lead slugs sang past his head, forcing him to duck and move again. Yep, there was more than one shooter on this side. Goddam, he thought, hope to hell there ain't a damned army of 'em.

Lighthorse could see shadowy movement, but nothing definite enough to shoot at. Damn those trees. Not a clear field of fire. He saw more movement, but he decided to hold his fire until he had a good target. They didn't know where he was, but if he fired, they'd know.

It was quiet again. Come daylight, we're in for a hell of a fight, Lighthorse thought. I hope to hell there ain't a damned army of 'em.

Sammy's knees were painfully cramped, and he had to move again, had to straighten his legs. Had to do it before daylight when the all-out attack would come. He felt that he was taking a chance when he climbed to the bottom of the arroyo, stretched his legs, and took a few steps in each direction to work the cramps out. Then he climbed back to the same place.

Daylight was slow in coming. At first it was only a few pale, pink streaks above the jagged horizon where the sun reflected off some low, thin clouds. Gradually, the pink turned to red, casting a glow over the treetops, and eventually, the rocky ground under the short, twisted trees became more visible. Sammy saw a man over there. A man with a shapeless black hat and baggy denim pants held up with suspenders. He drew a bead on the man, thinking it was best to knock down as many of them as they could before the real battle started. But the man walked behind a tree.

A gunshot came from across the arroyo. Looking back, Sammy saw Lighthorse duck and lever in another round, then move to his right. Hope you got one of the sons of bitches, Sammy thought. Out of the corner of his eye he saw something move. Two men were over there in front of him, behind the trees, only their heads and shoulders showing. They were looking for him.

The party was about to begin.

Five

Lighthorse saw the man step boldly from behind a tree, then jump back just as he fired. The son of a bitch was trying to draw fire, and it worked. They knew where he was now—approximately. The next time he showed his head, they'd see him.

Well, he had to show himself. That or duck his head and wait to get shot.

Carefully, he moved to his right, raised his head again. A rifle slug knocked his gray high-crown hat half off his head. Instead of ducking instinctively, he looked to see where the shot had come from. The shooter was behind a tree, only his right arm showing, levering in another round. Lighthorse aimed quickly and squeezed the trigger.

Goddam. Knocked some chips off the tree, but the man was still standing. Lighthorse moved again.

Across the arroyo, Sammy aimed at a man's shoulder and fired. He watched with satisfaction as the man spun half around and fell. "That makes three less," he muttered.

Then lead came his way, spanging off the rocks, whistling near his head, forcing him to pull his head down. There were two more over there.

The sons of bitches had brought every killer in the territory with them, he thought.

Mrs. Henry Wilcox didn't know what to do. She'd been advised to stay down, but she couldn't just hide her head and let two men try to fight off a gang of killers. If they were shot dead, she would be, too. Without them, she'd be an easy victim. The gold would be gone. She remembered the last gunfight she'd been in. Scared mostly to death. But she'd managed to shoot anyway. When Henry was wounded, she'd tried to help him, but he'd ordered her to keep shooting. Maybe a miracle would happen, he'd said. A miracle did happen. If she kept shooting, maybe another miracle would come along.

Gripping her rifle, she climbed up beside Sammy.

"Hey," Sammy said, giving her only a glance. "Get back. Stay back. We don't need you yet. Be ready to defend yourself if they get down there."

"I thought maybe I could at least shoot in their direction."

"And get yourself shot? No. No, ma'am. Go back."

As she watched, Sammy took quick aim and squeezed the trigger of his rifle. She raised up and fired without aiming. Sammy gave her an angry glance, then turned his attention to the field ahead of him. No one moved. He watched, afraid to blink. "Come on out and fight," he muttered.

Lighthorse saw another shoulder, then a face. This time he took two seconds to aim. His rifle cracked, the recoil pounding his shoulder.

A man staggered from behind a tree, then fell onto his back. "The odds are looking better," Lighthorse said aloud.

As Sammy watched, he saw a man running, running away. He took quick aim and fired, but the man was running through the trees. Mrs. Wilcox saw no one, but she, too, fired. Then two men were running away.

Quiet again.

After a minute the woman asked, "Are they gone?"

"Shh. Try not to make a sound. Just listen."

Still quiet. When he thought about it, Sammy had to admit to himself that the woman's rifle had helped. Though she hadn't hit anybody, hadn't even tried to, the killers knew there were two guns over here. Two of them hadn't liked the odds and had run. If two had run, then surely there were no more. Not on this side, anyway.

"Would you do something, Mrs. Wilcox?"

She answered with determination, "Yes."

"Keep low. Don't expose yourself, but go over to Lighthorse and ask if he has any idea what's happening on his side."

"Surely."

Without turning his head, he heard her grunt, heard her shoes scraping the ground as she climbed down to the bottom of the arroyo. He kept his eyes wide open, watching everything, afraid to blink. Soon she was back.

"He said they're still there somewhere. Their horses are there. He said they might be planning a mass assault, and to stay ready."

"He's probably right."

The attack came. Rapid gunfire poured deadly lead into the ground near Lighthorse's head and whined over the arroyo. He fired, levered, fired. They were moving out there, keeping behind the trees as much as they could, but coming closer. Eventually one of their bullets would find him. But he, by God, wasn't going to sell his life cheap. He had to show his head and shoulders to do it, but he returned the fire as fast as he could. Soon he would have to reload, and then he was dead.

Across the gully, Sammy heard the battle, knew they were throwing everything they had at Lighthorse, knew his partner needed help. But if he went to help, would they attack from this side?

Damn, he muttered, if they had that much firepower, the three people in the gulch didn't have a chance.

Nothing was happening over here. Lighthorse needed help. Sammy had to make a decision.

"I hate to ask this of you, ma'am, but I've got to go over there and help Lighthorse. Would you keep your eyes on the terrain in front of us? If you see anything, fire a shot, and one of us will come back here."

"Yes. I will."

Sure, he thought, as he scrambled down the embankment, one of us will come back. If one of us is still alive.

Bullets were kicking up dirt in Lighthorse's face, and a slug picked at his right shirtsleeve. The only way to stop them was to hit one of them. He couldn't just shoot at them; he had to take aim and shoot them. Taking aim meant showing himself for at least two seconds, making a target of himself. He had no choice.

Lighthorse raised up long enough to aim at a man and squeeze the trigger. But at the same instant he'd fired, a bullet splintered a rock near his face, peppering his face with fragments. "Son of a bitch," he muttered, levering again. When he squeezed the trigger, the hammer tripped with only a click.

He ducked, jerked a box of cartridges from a shirt

pocket and started reloading as fast as his fingers would work. He couldn't reload fast enough.

"I'm as good as dead now," he muttered to himself. "Great spirits be kind."

Then another gun opened up beside him. Glancing to his left, he saw Sammy aiming and firing. White teeth flashing in a grin, the Indian said, "Pour it on 'em, pale face."

Sammy saw a man running toward him, rapidly firing a six-shooter. His shots were damned close. Sammy aimed at the middle of the man's chest, fired. The man stumbled and fell facedown.

"Minus another one," he muttered.

Now Lighthorse was shooting again. Sammy pulled his head down long enough to look back across the arroyo. The woman was still there, unhurt.

"Give 'em hell," he said, rising up, looking for a target.

But no more shots were coming from out there. Lighthorse stopped shooting. The two partners looked at each other. The Indian had a half-dozen small spots of blood on his cheeks, but no serious wounds. They heard horses snorting, heard hoofbeats. They listened.

"Reckon they gave up, white eyes?"

"Don't know, blanket ass. What do you think?"

"I think I ain't gonna go over there and look around. Not yet, anyhow."

"I'm gonna go back to the other side and keep watch."

"If there's no sign of 'em in, oh, say, two or three days, then maybe I'll go have what you white men call a looksee."

"I ain't gonna wait that long. I'm hungry."

Still grinning, Lighthorse said, "White man always hungry."

"If we cook some bacon, you'll gobble down your share."

"You betchem."

Mrs. Wilcox heard him coming, and watched him climb up beside her. "Was anyone hurt?"

"Naw. Lighthorse's got some blood on his face where some pieces of rock hit him, but he's not hurt."

She sighed, "Thank heavens."

"Any sign of anything over there?"

"I haven't seen anything at all."

"They probably gave up and left. We hit at least four of 'em. I don't know how many are left, but I'm guessing they decided the price was too high for your gold."

"I don't feel sorry for them. They must be the ones who killed my husband."

"Why don't you go down and fix something to eat. Build a fire and fry some bacon and make some coffee."

"All right."

Sammy kept watch until he saw a gray fox come out of the elder brush, sniff at a spot of blood, then turn and go back. That was a good sign. When Mrs. Wilcox yelled that breakfast was ready, he yelled at his partner.

"See anything, Lighthorse?"

"Nothing but a coyote."

"They're gone, then. I'm coming over."

They decided Sammy would eat while Lighthorse kept watch; then Lighthorse would eat.

"We've got to get going as quick as we can," Sammy said. "When we leave here, we'll soon be down on the prairie and better targets. We'll have to keep going 'til dark."

"We've got water in the canteens, but there's no water in these parts for the animals."

"We'll surely come to some water sometime today."

"There's a sump over northwest of here called Horse Springs. It's out of our way, but it could be the only water we'll see 'til we get into the Datils."

"It's down on the prairie?"

"Yeah. No place to hide."

"Well, I don't wanta cross this prairie without water."

After breakfast, when they rode out of the shallow end of the arroyo, the woman asked, "Are we going to do anything about the bodies?"

The partners looked at each other. Lighthorse said, "Indians pick up their dead."

"Outlaws have no honor. I don't feel much like digging graves, and we can't pack 'em out."

"Leave 'em."

The woman asked, "Do you think we should report this to the law?"

"Yeah, if we see them," Lighthorse said. "I'm not going far out of my way to do it."

"We'd have to go to Socorro or Belen to find a sheriff," Sammy said. "Then we'd have to come back here and show him the bodies, and then we'd have to stick around for a coroner's inquest or something, and we'd never get to Albuquerque."

"Oh," she said. "I didn't think about that."

"We can just keep quiet about it," Sammy said.

They rode out of the Elk Mountains onto the Plains of San Agustin and turned in a westerly direction. The country was mostly flat but with a few low hills. Ahead of them, far ahead, the Datil Mountains were a blue, sawtooth line on the horizon. Green bayonetlike leaves of yucca stuck up everywhere. Sagebrush and rabbit brush grew on the gentle slopes. Cholla cactus spread its arms up between the yucca. The travelers rode at a slow trot on the prairie, and kept at that gait most of the morning.

When they saw a small clump of willows a half-mile ahead, Lighthorse suddenly reined up. "I smell smoke," he said. "That there is Horse Springs, and the smoke is coming from a cooking fire."

"The question is," Sammy said, reining up beside him, "are they white or Indian?"

"Another question, if they're white, are they honest?"

Shaking his head, Sammy allowed, "When there's a hundred pounds of gold at stake, there ain't any honest men."

"We could turn north and stay away from there. What do you think?"

"The horses need water, and it looks like a long way to those mountains."

"All right, let's get a little closer." Lighthorse touched boot heels to his horse's sides and rode on at a walk. Sammy and the woman followed. Five hundred yards from the willows, the Indian stopped again.

"Something ain't right. I know—unless they're asleep over there—they've seen us. They don't want us to see who they are."

"It's too late to run. If they want to rob us, they can catch us before we get to the Datils."

"Let's get down and walk. Keep the horses safe."

Both men dismounted and handed their reins to the woman. "Stay here, Mrs. Wilcox," Sammy said, "until we find out who's over there."

Voice strained, she said, "Oh, my God. No more shooting. Please God, no more."

The partners walked, eyes straining, keeping ten paces apart, ready to hit the ground.

Six

When they were a hundred yards from the willows, they stopped and looked at each other.

"They're white men," Sammy said. "I can see two of 'em."

"White, and waiting for us to come closer."

Dropping onto one knee, rifle ready, Sammy said, "I can wait, too."

Lighthorse also got down on one knee. "I feel like I've got a target painted on my shirt," he said.

"Yeah, me, too. I wish somebody would do something." Sammy glanced back at the woman. She was standing on the ground, holding bridle reins and lead ropes in each hand, watching intently.

"Somebody's moving."

A man stepped out of the tall grass and willows. He was carrying a rifle in his hands and a six-gun in a holster on his right side. He hollered, "Hey over there. I'm Sheriff Elmer Pogue of Socorro County. Come forward and identify yourself."

Without standing, Sammy yelled, "Come closer, Sheriff, and identify yourself."

"I'm coming. There are four of us and we can outshoot you. Keep your fingers off of those triggers." He walked toward them, walked without fear. "Like I said, you're in the gunsights of three good shots right now. You might as well stand up."

Now he was close enough that the partners could see the badge pinned to the pocket of his blue broadcloth shirt. He was short, stout, with a dirty gray hat and pant legs stuffed inside high-top boots. Sammy stood. "We have to be careful, Sheriff."

"Can't blame you for that. Is that a woman over yonder?"

"Yessir. Call your men out so we can put down these guns."

Sheriff Pogue half-turned and waved. Three men stepped out of the willows, all carrying rifles. "They're deputies of mine. We trailed some horse thieves plumb over the Mogollons and lost 'em. We think they sold 'em to the Apaches. When we saw you comin' we thought you might be outlaws, and we tried to stay out of sight 'til you come close enough that we could see you better. Where are you folks headed?"

"Albuquerque."

They were joined by the three deputies, all wearing stockmen's hats and boots, and all armed with rifles and six-guns. Sammy studied them carefully. They didn't look threatening. Then he noticed that the sheriff and his deputies were studying Lighthorse, frowning. The Indian met their gaze without flinching.

Sammy said, "He's a Muache Ute, and he was a scout for the Sixth Cavalry until a couple of weeks ago."

"Can he talk English?"

Lighthorse answered, "Very well, Sheriff."

"Oh. Well, then, call the woman over. There's water,

but we're just about out of grub. We run out of coffee yesterday." ·

"I'll go help her with the animals," Lighthorse said, and he turned and walked in her direction.

"We've got coffee," Sammy said, "and maybe more beans and side meat than we need. If you men are hungry, we'll share it with you."

One of the deputies said, "I could shore use some java."

"We just fried some salt pork, and the fire's still hot," said another.

They all waited until Lighthorse and Mrs. Wilcox came up, leading the horses and mule. The sheriff introduced himself, but not his deputies. She was pleased to meet him, she said. Then they all walked over to the willows.

Clear, cool water bubbled out of the ground among the willow bushes, and the animals drank their fill. The lawmen's horses were hobbled nearby, finding a few blades of grass in the rabbit brush. Sammy and Lighthorse off-saddled their horses and mule and let them graze on whatever they could find. A few dead willows provided fuel for the fire, though other travelers had, over the years, cut down some of the bushes. One of the deputies helped Mrs. Wilcox feed the fire and put the coffeepot on. The deputy, a thin young man with a scraggly moustache, couldn't keep his eyes off her. Her baggy clothes and wide-brim hat couldn't hide the fact that she was a handsome woman, slim and shapely. His eyes followed her every move.

She smiled nervously at him, then deliberately avoided looking his way.

The sheriff asked, "Would you mind telling me, ma'am, why you all are traveling by this route?"

Not knowing what to say, she looked to Sammy. He answered with the truth, and ended by telling about burying her husband at Fort Bayard. He didn't mention the gunfight in the Elk Mountains.

"I'm terrible sorry, ma'am. It must be awful for you."

She busied herself pouring coffee into tin cups. But the sheriff's curiosity wasn't satisfied. "If they was robbers, what was it they was after?"

Again, she didn't know how to answer. Putting the coffeepot down, she said with embarrassment, "If you gentlemen will excuse me a moment . . ."

"Oh, of course, ma'am."

She pushed her way through the willows.

Everyone else was sitting on the ground, sipping scalding hot black coffee. Everyone but Sheriff Pogue. He stood with his feet apart, thumbs hooked inside his gunbelt. Now he turned his attention to Sammy. "Where did you all start from?"

"Fort Bayard," Sammy answered.

"Oh, I get it. She hired you two to accompany her to Albuquerque."

"Yes sir."

"Did you come out of the Elk Mountains or did you come up the west slopes of the Black Range?"

There was no way to answer that without asking for trouble. If he admitted they'd come over the Elks, and if those dead men were found and reported to Sheriff Pogue, the sheriff would know they'd had something to do with killing them. If he said they'd come up the west side of the Black Range, the sheriff would ask what they were doing this far west. And if he told about the gun battle and the dead men, they'd be escorted to Socorro, and they'd have to stay there until the sheriff completed an investigation. That would take a week at least. They could even be locked up in the guard house.

He had to say something. He didn't know what to say. Then it occurred to him that he didn't have to say anything. He was a civilian now.

Looking over the rim of his coffee cup, Sammy said, "Sheriff, have you ever been in the army?"

"No, can't say I have. What's that got to do with anything?"

"Well, Lighthorse and I, we mustered out at Fort Union two-three weeks ago. In the army, an enlisted man never questions his superiors. When an officer says 'Frog,' we don't ask why; we jump. When an officer asks us a question, we answer immediately. When we get out of bed in the morning, we don't get dressed until an officer decides what the uniform of the day will be. If an officer decides to have the men fall out and do ten pushups before breakfast, hundreds of men fall out and do ten pushups. You're not a free man in the army."

Sheriff Pogue was staring at him, wondering what he was coming to. Sammy swallowed a lump in his throat and continued. "Me, when I mustered out and went to Santa Fe, I stood on the street a long time before I convinced myself I was free. I felt like a man just out of prison must feel. I could go anywhere I wanted to go, wear any kind of clothes I wanted to wear. And"— he met the sheriff's gaze head-on—"I didn't have to say 'Sir' to anybody, and I didn't have to answer anybody's questions."

Everyone was staring at him without speaking. Sammy finished his coffee and put the cup on the ground. The woman came back, sat on her feet and picked up her coffee cup. When she noticed that everyone was staring at Sammy, a puzzled look came over her face.

Finally, Sheriff Pogue shifted his weight from one foot to the other and said, "Well, I ain't seen nor heard nothing that'd give me cause for suspicion. We'll be leaving. Hope to get home before dark tomorrow night."

Alone again, they finished their meal and put out the fire. When canteens were filled and animals watered and saddled, Sammy said, "You know this country better than I do, pardner, should we climb the Datils and go over the divide where there's bound to be a stream of some kind, or head around to the west where the traveling is easier?"

"Well," Lighthorse took his time answering, "it's like you said; if we go over the Datils, we won't die of thirst, and there's good grazing up there for the animals. But since we've already come this far west, we can get to Albuquerque faster by going around the Datils. The nearest water that I know of is a draw called Red Creek that sometimes has water in it. We'd get there about this time tomorrow. Maybe sooner if we strike a trot."

"What do you say, Mrs. Wilcox?" Sammy asked.

Shrugging with both hands out, palms up, she said, "I have to leave those decisions to you gentlemen."

Lighthorse said, "You're a corporal, and I rank about the same as a buck private. You decide."

"I ain't a corporal, and you ain't a private. There ain't any rank. But if it's up to me, we'll take the easiest route. If I'm wrong, you can kick me."

Grinning, Lighthorse said, "If I got kicked every time I was wrong, I'd be a mess of bruises."

The sun was past its peak and on its downward slide when they left Horse Springs. They rode through more sagebrush, rabbit brush, yucca and cane cactus. A rattlesnake buzzed its warning off to their right, and Lighthorse drew his six-gun, then holstered it again. "I hate those sons of, uh, I've seen what they can do to a man, and I swore once I'd kill every one I saw. But the sound of a gunshot goes a long way, and there's no use drawing attention."

They rode past the eroded foothills of the Mangas Mountains and continued north. As the sun was about to slide behind the Mangases, they began crossing arroyos, deep draws and talus slopes at the foot of the Datils. Everything was dry. In a wide draw where the spring snowmelt and summer rains had left the grass more plentiful, they stopped for the night.

"These animals ain't thirsty yet," Lighthorse said, "but they might be feeling a little thirst before morning, and they might leave us to look for water."

"Yeah, they can travel with hobbles, but maybe if we let 'em drag long halter ropes, they won't travel far."

While Sammy hobbled the horses and mule, Lighthorse chopped some piñon and scrub cedars for firewood. "I've been watching," he said to Mrs. Wilcox, "and I'm pretty sure there's no other human anywhere near. After tomorrow morning we'll have to be more careful."

They ate their fill of fried side meat, dried fruit and canned vegetables. Then, just before dark, the woman went in one direction up the draw, the two men in the other direction.

"She said two hundred bucks apiece," Sammy said. "That's more than six months' army pay."

"That's more than six-and-a-half months' pay."

"Well, if that gold we're packing is the pure stuff, she won't miss four hundred dollars."

"What do you wanta do when we get paid off?"

"I dunno. Go back to the Pinos Altos and look for gold?"

"That's what we started out to do."

"I don't know of any other way to get rich. Maybe we can find a pile of gold like that crazy German did."

"Huh," Lighthorse snorted, "the only piles we'll ever find are the bleeding, itching kind."

With a chuckle, Sammy said, "Well, we can look 'til we run out of money; then we can always re-up."

"Yeah, there's that. But like I said before, I wanta see what it's like to be what you called a free civilian."

"If Sheriff Pogue gets wind of those dead men back there, he'll know who to look for."

"Uh-huh. Then we won't be so free. And civilians or not, we'll have to answer some questions."

"Damned if there ain't always something to worry about."

Seven

In the shadow of the Datil Mountains, the travelers could see the sun shining on the plains west of them as they loaded the pack animals and saddled their horses. By the time they rode out of the wide draw the sun had cleared the high hills to the east and was spreading its warmth all over the land.

"Figure we'll get to that Red Creek before dark?" Sammy asked.

"Ought to get there by noon, or shortly after."

They rode silently, the Datils looming to their right and the plains to their left. Late in the morning they were beyond the mountains and could see nothing but the Plains of San Agustin ahead. They were traveling in a shuffling trot with Lighthorse in the lead.

Sammy's mind was back in the army, Company M. In most of the patrols he'd ridden with, it was Lighthorse and at least one other Indian scout who had taken the lead. Some believed the Indians had stronger senses than white men, but most knew it wasn't so. There were white scouts who could track, see, hear and smell as well as any Indian, men who had lived in the wilds of the frontier west for many years. Sammy wasn't one of them.

Samual J. Collins was raised in a Chicago orphanage, where he learned early in life to fight with his fists. It was fight or be bullied. Though he was an inch under six feet tall, he was a lightweight, and had to be quick with his fists to earn any respect from his peers. He was quick, and he was determined enough to take a beating and keep fighting. He'd never held a gun in his hands until he enlisted in the infantry. First, he'd run away from the orphanage at sixteen and worked his way south just to see the country. He'd milked cows until his hands ached, and cut hay with a scythe until his arms and back ached. He'd picked cotton and chopped the Johnsongrass out of rows of growing cotton with a hoe. He'd cleaned roosting houses until his nose and throat burned with the stink.

"Hell, son," he was told by a man he'd met in a Louisville flophouse, "if you wanta see the country, join the army and go out west and fight Indians." Young Collins was seventeen, but claimed to be eighteen when he enlisted in the Thirty-seventh United States Infantry. And when he was assigned to Company C on the Chama River in the Territory of New Mexico, he was excited and looking forward to some adventure. It didn't turn out that way.

Private Collins was assigned to work with the post surgeon and help take care of the sick and wounded. There were no wounded. Company C stayed in garrison. There were the sick, though, and Private Collins had to sop up blood after surgery, carry out shit buckets, clean up vomit, and snap to attention every time an officer came in sight. Every day was drudgery, with guard duty, foot patrols, and inspection after inspection.

The day his enlistment was up he took his honorable

discharge, went to Fort Bayard and joined the Sixth Cavalry. He was assigned a horse, a gentle sorrel gelding with a number instead of a name, and he was instructed on how to take care of it.

"Shit," an old non-com advised him, "the damned army takes better care of its horses than it does its men." That was fine with Private Collins. He liked horses, and taking care of them was better than taking care of sick men. His big disappointment in Company M of the Sixth came when he spent four days on his first patrol without seeing an Indian. But the disappointment didn't last.

A large band of Chiricahuas had left a reservation in Arizona and come back to New Mexico, a land they had occupied for several generations and knew better than any white man. They hated whites and Mexicans, and their goal was to kill as many as they could, steal everything they could and destroy what wasn't worth stealing. Company M engaged the enemy many times, killed some Apaches and lost some troopers. In the first engagement Private Collins was so scared he couldn't stop shaking. But with unsteady hands he managed to fire his breech-loading carbine, flip up the loading gate, reload and fire again.

He was horrified the first time he took aim at a barechested Apache, squeezed the trigger and saw his target fall off his horse and lie still. But then an Indian bullet grazed his left shoulder, leaving a raw red welt, and for a time he forgot everything else in the world except how to shoot and fight.

He'd learned something in that first engagement: The Indians were damned good soldiers. They knew how to fight. They were brave and daring. And the white troopers had to either learn to fight the Indian way or be chased out of the territory.

The Sixth Cavalry learned. Private Collins learned. Private Collins survived. He was promoted to corporal.

Then Company M moved north to Fort Union, where the troopers took the place of a Negro company that was transferred to somewhere in Texas. Only occasional patrols left Fort Union to engage the Apaches. Most patrols went south to the Mangas Mountains, the Black Range and the Mogollons, but a few went north to take on the Jicarillas. Most battles were short, but bloody, with more Indians killed than troopers. But troopers were killed and wounded, and Corporal Collins, with his experience in the Thirty-seventh Infantry, was often ordered to help care for the wounded.

It was in the Jawbone Mountains up north that he first saw the Ute Indian named Lighthorse. The young Indian wasn't far from death, and Corporal Collins was ordered to keep him alive.

Back at Fort Union a surgeon took over the responsibility, but a trust and friendship had developed between the two young men. The Indian made it understood that he wanted to learn English, and Corporal Collins was his first teacher.

Now, as Sammy Collins looked at the Indian's back, sitting straight and tall in a civilian saddle, he knew the friendship was something he'd value for the rest of his life.

At noon, Lighthorse had to admit that Red Creek was farther away than he'd reckoned, and the partners decided to keep going without stopping to rest and eat.

"These brutes are too thirsty now to eat," Sammy

allowed, "and if we keep going, we ought to get to that creek in a few hours."

Riding at a shuffling trot, they went on. The horses and mule were moving woodenly, heads down. When Lighthorse pointed to the west, Sammy looked to see what he was pointing at. Through heat waves he saw the figures on horseback, away over there, about twenty of them.

"Indians?" he asked.

"Yep."

"They've seen us, you can bet, but they don't seem to be interested in us."

"Women and kids."

"That means there's some men somewhere around."

"Probably ahead of 'em. I'd guess the men are in the Mangases hunting meat, and the women and kids expect to meet them there."

"If the men had seen us, they'd be hunting us instead of wild game."

"They didn't see us, but the women will tell 'em about us. Maybe by that time we'll be too far away for them to fool with."

"I just hope we don't meet any Apaches at Red Creek."

The horses and mule smelled water a half hour before they came to Red Creek. The mule, being a hybrid, couldn't bray like a donkey, but it tried. What came out of it was a half bray, half scream.

"Funny thing about mules," Sammy said. "Some can bray and some can't."

"They can sure make themselves heard. If anybody is camped up there, they'll know we're coming."

"Oh, well, they'd know anyway."

They had the creek, what there was of it, to themselves. It was only a mud hole in a shallow draw, with a few willows growing along it. "It seems to me," Sammy said, "where there's willows there's water."

With the shovel from the pack panniers, he dug in the mud until water seeped up into the hole. Brown, dirty water. The partners allowed the pack animals to drink first, then unloaded them while the saddle horses drank, crowding each other, their heads together and their knees bent to reach the water.

Sammy pulled them away long enough for seepage to fill the hole again.

While the animals grazed on crested wheatgrass, hopping from clump to clump with their forefeet hobbled, the three humans chewed fried side meat left over from breakfast and dried fruit. They saved the fresh water remaining in their canteens and swallowed the brown water. The woman made a wry face.

"At least it's wet and we won't die of dehydration," Sammy commented.

Lighthorse walked out of the draw and took a long look around. "Nobody in sight. This ain't a favorite watering hole."

"We've been down the west side of the Rio Grande," Sammy said, "and if I remember right, there's a creek or small river ahead called Puerco."

"Yep. If we go straight east, we'll come to the Rio Grande and the road going north and south; but Puerco River ain't much farther, and we can camp there out of sight of the road."

"I'd say it's a long day's ride from here."

"How much farther to Albuquerque?" the woman asked.

"Another day from Puerco. Two more days from here." Sammy noticed then the tired lines in her face and the way she sat slumped over. "You can make it, Mrs. Wilcox."

"Yes," she said, straightening her shoulders, "I can make it."

"Did you say you're going to St. Louis from Albuquerque?"

"Yes. That's where Henry and I came from. We both have family there. I . . ." She looked down, eyes sad. "I'll have to tell his family, his brother and two sisters. His parents have passed on."

Sammy sympathized. "It's a darned shame."

"Yes." She squared her shoulders again.

"Will you leave right away?"

"I don't think so. I'm not looking forward to a long trip in a stagecoach, and I'd like to rest a few days. When I get to Denver I can travel in a railroad coach. That will be more comfortable."

"How'd you happen to come to this territory?" Then Sammy added quickly, "It's none of my business. You don't have to answer."

She answered anyway. "Gold. You've heard, haven't you, how men will do anything, suffer any hardship, for a chance at striking it rich? Henry and his brother Jonathan were grain brokers. One bad year was all it took to ruin them financially. Henry, like many others, heard about men getting rich in the gold fields in Colorado and in southern New Mexico Territory. We heard a lot about Colorado, but little about New Mexico. So while most gold seekers went straight west, Henry decided to come southwest. Perhaps he would be among the first to prospect in the Black Range."

"But . . . ?" Sammy was clearly puzzled.

"You're wondering why I came along?" A wry smile pulled up one corner of her mouth. "I've wondered that many times myself. But the answer is simple. I . . ." She almost couldn't say it, but she forced it out. "I loved my husband very much, and I didn't want us to be separated. Where he went, I wanted to go. Insisted on going."

Lighthorse said nothing, just listened.

She talked on; "We stayed awhile at Kingston, but the town, the tent city, rather, was swarming with prospectors. We went on west to a tiny settlement named Buckhorn where gold had been discovered. Henry staked a claim on Apache Creek and, wonder of wonders, found color, as he called it. He made sure the dust he collected in his pan was the genuine article, then built a sluice box. It took four years, but eventually he collected enough dust and nuggets that he believed he could finance a new business of some kind in St. Louis. We started out in the dark of night, hoping the robbers wouldn't see us, but . . . you saw what happened."

She stopped talking, brought her knees up, crossed her arms on her knees and put her head on her arms. Lighthorse stood and walked out of the draw to where he could study the country around them.

Finally, Sammy said quietly, "We're gonna get you and your gold to Albuquerque, Mrs. Wilcox. You can bet on that." Right then Sammy was full of admiration for Mrs. Wilcox, and he would have done anything for her.

She raised her head and forced a smile. "You've been wonderful."

It was about noon the next day when they again saw other humans. They didn't like what they saw.

Eight

They'd been traveling at a slow but steady trot since first light, hoping to reach the Puerco River long before dark. As usual, it was Lighthorse who spotted them. Six, coming at a gallop. The Indian stopped, twisted in his saddle with his right hand on his horse's rump, and watched them. Then he looked at his partner.

"Oooh boy," he said. "They must've made it to Magdalena somehow, picked up some partners and fresh horses and figured out where we'd be."

Looking around desperately, Sammy said, "And there ain't a defiladed area in sight."

"Arroyo, civilian."

"Whatever, there ain't any. We'd better strike a full gallop. Mrs. Wilcox, it's time to whip your pony into a run."

Lighthorse said, "I don't know where we're running to, but let's ride."

They got their animals into a lope. The mule would trot all day; but it wasn't used to running with a load on its back, and it pulled on the lead rope. Sammy wrapped the packhorse's lead rope around his saddle horn, rode alongside the mule's rump and whipped it with the ends of his bridle reins. The woman's sorrel horse was running well, and she was leaning forward over the saddle horn. Her broad-brim hat had blown off her head, but the thong under her chin kept it from blowing away. Her dark hair was streaming behind her, and her divided skirt was whipping high on her legs.

Looking back, Sammy could see the men gaining. He yelled at Lighthorse, "We're gonna have to take a stand someplace."

"I'm looking for a place."

A rifle cracked behind them, but the bullet fell short. Sammy wanted to draw his six-gun, twist in his saddle and fire a shot back at them. Aim high, and maybe get lucky. But he had to keep slapping the mule's rump.

They rode, trying to urge the pack animals to run faster. The horses and mule had to dodge yucca and cane cactus. The riders behind them were getting closer. Soon they'd be in rifle range. The three crossed a shallow draw, but it was too shallow to be any protection.

Again a rifle cracked, but again the bullet didn't come close. It's hard to aim a rifle from the back of a running horse, Sammy thought. They'll have to get a lot closer.

It was a horse race. The three riders in the lead were at a disadvantage with their pack animals, and they looked desperately for an arroyo, someplace where they could fort up. There was nothing.

More gunfire came from behind them. They could tell from the sound that their pursuers were gaining. Gaining fast. They rode across a narrow valley dotted with piñon and scrub cedars. Still no cover. Their animals were tiring. The race would soon be over. A bullet would hit them or one of the animals. That would do it.

Company M of the Sixth had trained their horses to

lie down, and the troopers had practiced squatting behind the downed horses, using them for a fortress.
Though the army was often accused of taking better
care of its horses than its men, the Sixth was willing
to sacrifice horses rather than troopers.

But these horses weren't trained to lie down. They
would go down only if shot down. The three travelers
needed the horses, all of them.

Ahead the ground rose in a gentle but long swell. An
uphill run would take it all out of the animals. Unless
there was something up there to use for a barricade, the
chase would soon be over. Six well-armed killers against
two men and a woman would make it a one-sided battle.

Well, by God, Sammy and Lighthorse would make
them pay. Some of those six wouldn't profit from the
killing and robbing.

Shots were coming every few seconds now. Coming
closer. Lighthorse twisted in his saddle and fired two
rounds from his six-gun, hoping to hit something. The
six kept coming, gaining.

Sammy shouted, "When we get to the top of this hill,
let's stop and take a stand. These horses can't go much
farther."

"That's what we'll have to do."

"I'm sorry, Mrs. Wilcox. We're doing the best we
can."

She didn't answer, only grimaced.

The horses and mule had run as far as they could
run when they topped the rise. Sammy pulled up and
started to get down. Stopped suddenly. Stared. Ahead
was something they hadn't expected to see.

"Well, what the hell . . . ?"

"Cattle," Lighthorse said. "A lot of cattle. A big herd. And cowboys."

Dumbfounded, Sammy said, "Well, I'll be damned. Hope they're armed."

Flashing a grin, Lighthorse said, "I never saw an unarmed cowboy." He fired a shot in the air to draw attention. The mounted men ahead looked back.

"Let's get down there." Sammy socked his horse's sides with spurless boot heels and at the same time slapped the mule's rump. Lighthorse and the woman urged their horses into a slow, tired gallop.

Behind them, the six hooligans topped the hill and started down. But by then the cowboys, about ten of them, had spotted the outlaws, saw what was happening, and gathered on the near end of the herd. They all drew their six-guns, watching, ready to shoot.

Lighthorse looked back, grinned, white teeth flashing. "They gave up. They don't wanta shoot it out with a crew of cowboys."

The three allowed their horses to slow to a trot, then to a walk. The animals' sides were heaving, and they walked with their heads down. Two of the cowboys rode toward them, still gripping their six-guns. Lighthorse holstered his gun to show that he was through shooting. When only twenty feet separated them, the cowboys reined up. The one to speak was middle-aged, thin, with a walrus moustache and a high-crown, flat-brim gray hat.

"Howdy." He touched his hat brim and nodded at the woman. "Ma'am."

"How do you do," she said.

The cowboy's squinty eyes settled on Lighthorse. The Indian met his gaze, but said nothing. Sammy spoke,

"He's a Ute and he's been an army scout. He's on our side."

"Oh." The thin one turned his eyes to Sammy. "If it ain't too much bother, would you mind tellin' us what's goin' on."

Half-turning to look back, Sammy said, "That bunch is determined to rob us. We've tangled with some of them before. They got some reinforcements and fresh horses somewhere and they tried again."

"Uh-huh." The squinty eyes studied Sammy, the woman, Lighthorse, then turned back to Sammy. "And you was outnumbered and you had to run for it."

Nodding, Sammy said, "Correct. These horses have run about as far as they can. We were ready to get down and shoot it out the best we could. You all probably saved our lives."

"Can he talk English?"

Lighthorse answered, "Yes sir. I can speak it, read it and write it."

"Oh. Wal, where'd you all come from?"

"We started from Fort Bayard and we're headed for Albuquerque."

"Unh." Looking up the hill, then back, the cowboy said, "My name is Amos Carter. I'm wagon boss for this outfit, the Z Slash from over on the Arizona border. We had a dry camp last night, and we're trying to get to the Puerco River before dark." He glanced at the afternoon sun. "I ain't been in this country before, and I ain't sure we're gonna make it. These beefs and our remuda ain't tasted water since yestidy mornin', and I hate to make another dry camp; but I reckon we'll have to."

Sammy introduced them. "I'm Samual Collins, this

is Mrs. Wilcox and my partner is Lighthorse Jones. Lighthorse and I mustered out of the Sixth Cavalry a few weeks ago."

Lighthorse said, "We've been over this country, and I'd guess the river is six or eight miles north by northeast. You're headed in the right direction."

"Wal, I'm glad to hear that. Maybe we can make 'er by sundown or right soon after. I'd druther cross rivers in the evenin', but maybe that 'un ain't too deep."

"It's not deep at all," Lighthorse said. "In fact, there can't be much water in it this time of year."

"Uh-huh. Wal, them gents up there ain't gonna lock horns with us. You all can ride along with us if you want to, or go on ahead. A herd of cattle don't move very fast."

The two partners looked at each other, at Mrs. Wilcox. Lighthorse said, "If we go on ahead, they'll see us. You can bet they're watching. They'll know where we're going."

"Yep," Sammy said, "and these horses can't stand another run today." Looking at the woman, he asked, "What do you think, Mrs. Wilcox?"

With a weak smile, she said, "I don't think I can stand another race either. And I'd do almost anything to prevent more shooting."

The two cowboys had just discovered what a handsome woman she was, and were looking at her with interest. Finally, Amos Carter said, "Our wagon is up there somewhere, and the cook is looking for a place to camp tonight. You sure it ain't more'n eight miles?"

"I'd bet on it."

"Wal then, I'll ride up to the wagon with you and tell the cook to keep goin'."

"If we had fresh mounts, we'd help you with the cattle," Sammy said. "Or try to."

The wagon boss pulled a sack of tobacco out of a shirt pocket and rolled a cigarette, holding his reins between two fingers. He took his right foot out of the stirrup long enough to raise his knee and tighten the denim of his pant leg, then struck a match on his outer thigh. His pant leg was streaked where he'd struck a hundred matches. The other cowboy, who hadn't spoken a word, rolled a smoke, too, but struck his match on the rawhide wrapped around his saddle horn.

After a few puffs, the wagon boss said, "We don't need any help. These beefs're purty well trail broke. You can help the cook if you want to, or just rest, whatever you wanta do. You're welcome to eat with us tonight." With just a flick of the reins he turned his horse around and rode toward the herd. Everyone followed.

As they rode, Sammy said, "I don't see any calves. Did you say these cattle are beeves?"

"All beefs. Eight hunnerd and eighty-eight of 'em. They're gonna feed a lot of folks in Albukirk. A buyer is s'posed to meet us at the river."

The cattle were spread over a good fifty acres, and now the wagon boss waved at his crew and yelled, "String 'em out. We're not too far from water now."

With yells, whistles and whirling catch ropes, the cowboys started pushing the cattle into a long line. The cattle were slobbering and moving slowly with their heads down.

"They'll walk faster when they get close enough to water to smell it," the wagon boss said. He touched spurs to his horse and rode at a trot around the herd. The other cowboy dropped back to help the crew. Ahead were two wagons with canvas tops, each pulled by four-horse teams.

When he trotted up to the lead wagon, Amos Carter slowed his horse to a walk and shouted at the wrinkled old man sitting on a high seat, handling the driving lines. "We'll keep 'er goin'. These folks say the river ain't more'n eight miles ahead." He had to shout to make himself heard over the creaking and rattling of the wagon and the trace chains.

The wrinkled face under a floppy black hat split into a grin. "Thas good news. I didn't wanta even think about another dry camp." He, too, looked first at the woman, then at the Indian.

The wagon boss said, "He knows this country."

"Thas good. I'm glad somebody does." He quit staring at Lighthorse.

"This is Mrs. Wilcox. She's a lady. They're headed for Albukirk. Don't get too far ahead of us, there's a bunch of gunnies back there that're up to no good."

"Is that what the ruckus was about?"

"Yeah. They won't attack us. There's too many of us. But don't get too far ahead."

"Yassir." The old man reached down and picked up a lever-action carbine. "But I ain't had a chancet to shoot this here Winchester for a couple of weeks. Let 'em come."

Nine

The wagon boss said, "These folks can ride along with you or git in one of the wagons or whatever they wanta do."

The wrinkled face turned to the woman. "Mizzuz Wilcox, my name is Andy. You can ride up here with me if you want to. I ain't presentable-lookin', but I'm a harmless ol' bat." He put the rifle back under the seat.

She smiled a genuine smile. "I appreciate that, Mr., uh, Andy, but I've grown accustomed to riding a horse."

"Whatever you say, ma'am. If you change your mind, holler, and I'll whoa this team for you."

"Thank you very much."

The wagon boss turned his horse around again and rode at a lope back to the herd. Off to the west was another herd, this one made up of about fifty horses, all being handled by one man.

"That has to be their remuda," Sammy said.

Nodding, Lighthorse commented, "It would take ten troopers to handle that many animals."

"I'd go over and help him, but I'm no cowboy and I'd probably just get in his way."

* * *

The Puerco River, when they reached it just at sundown, presented good news and bad news. The bad news was the river wasn't much more than a trickle in most places. Andy was the first to reach the water. "Hope I can fill the barrels and buckets afore them beefs get here. With them trompin' around this water won't be fit to drink for a long time."

The second wagon was driven by a teenage pimply-faced boy in a bill cap and brogan shoes. He climbed down from his wagon and began dipping water out of the stream and pouring it into a wooden barrel. Sammy and Lighthorse helped, dipping pots and pans. When the two barrels were full, the four of them carried them back to the chuck wagon. Lighthorse grabbed the axe from their pack panniers and got busy chopping buck brush for the cook's fire as Sammy unloaded the pack animals and unsaddled the horses.

While the animals rolled to scratch their sweating backs, the remuda stood in the water, horses crowding one another to get their broad lips into it. Then the cattle came at a trot, slobbering, hooking one another with their wide horns to get to the stream. The crew tried to bring them in at an angle, riding between them and the stream to keep them strung out along the bank. Cattle lined the river for a quarter mile.

The good news was an easy river crossing. At its deepest point the water wasn't more than knee-deep to a steer. Cowboys allowed their horses to drink, then rode across the muddy bank to keep cattle from wandering away after their thirst was sated.

Working by lantern light, Andy mixed biscuit dough and baked the biscuits in a heavy iron dutch oven which sat in the middle of the fire. While that was baking he patted some of the dough into pie pans and added dried apples. Biscuits done, he lifted the pot out of the fire and put in a pot of beans and a pot of beef stew left over from the night before.

The cattle were busy grazing on what grass they could find, and all but three of the cowboys unsaddled their horses, turned them into the remuda, caught some night horses, then sat cross-legged on the ground while they ate. The woman, Lighthorse and Sammy sat with them.

"This is the best meal I've had in a long time," Lighthorse said, as much to show everyone he could speak English as to compliment the cook.

"Wonderful," Mrs. Wilcox said around a mouthful.

The cowboys didn't want to stare at her, but they couldn't help sneaking glances now and then.

Meal over, most of the cowboys rolled cigarettes, leaned back against their bedrolls and talked. Three rode across the stream to relieve the nightherds.

"You say them gunsels intended to rob you?"

"Yeah," Sammy answered. "That's what they had planned, all right." He could almost see their minds working, wondering what these three had that was worth killing for. But they didn't ask, and no one volunteered the information. Sammy and Lighthorse didn't expect any trouble from the cowboy crew, but they slept near their tarp-covered pack boxes and panniers.

In the morning, they had to go on alone.

They soon picked up a trail that paralleled the Rio Grande, with Lighthorse going ahead, watching for ambushers. "If you hear a shot, look for cover," he said.

"There's a road across the river somewhere," Sammy said. "If we're attacked, we'll head for that and hope to find some help."

"If they're waiting for us, they're probably watching the road, in which case we might slip past 'em. And then maybe they're watching the road and this trail."

It was a hot summer day; but the trail was an easy one, and they kept their horses at a slow trot. At mid-afternoon they rode through an acre of buck brush and came to the outskirts of the big, sprawling town of Albuquerque. As they rode along dusty streets, lined with adobe and clapboard shacks, Mexican kids gathered to stare at them. The adults paid them little attention.

"Now that we're here, Mrs. Wilcox, where do you want to go?" Sammy asked.

"First to a good hotel. One with a safe, if there is such a thing. The banks are probably closed for the day, so I can't convert this gold to cash until tomorrow."

"If we're lucky," Lighthorse said, "no one will know what's in them pack boxes."

"I'll feel better when it's in a good strong safe."

"Me, too," Sammy said. "And I'll feel better yet after I've had a meal of good fresh beef and anything else but canned stuff and dried fruit."

Lighthorse said, "Let's look for a hotel for Mrs. Wilcox first. Ever been in this town before, Mrs. Wilcox?"

"No. When we, Henry and I, came to this territory we came through Texas and bypassed northern New Mexico."

"I've been here. I didn't stay long enough to see much of the town, but I did see some hotels. If we can find the plaza, we'll find the best hotel."

They found the plaza easily. It would have been impossible to miss, with its square block of benches, footpaths, and a bandstand. On one side, across a hard-packed dirt street, stood the most beautiful building either young man had ever seen. Made of stone and bricks with a tile roof, etched glass windows and many dormers, the San Felipe De Neri Church was about seventy-five years old. It had replaced an older one built centuries earlier. Stores, shops and restaurants of all kinds surrounded the plaza. And hotels. And saloons.

Riding up to the Coronado, which looked to be the biggest and finest hotel near the plaza, the woman dismounted sorely and went inside while the two young men stayed outside. When she came out, she said, "I've taken a room, and yes, they have a safe."

But when the proprietor, a round-faced man with a German accent, saw the two pack boxes, he shook his head. "There iss nod room for both uff dem. Mebbe one uff dem, but nod both."

"What we'll have to do, then," Lighthorse said, "is put everything in one box. Can we do that in your room, Mrs. Wilcox?"

"Of course."

Next stop for the men was a livery barn three blocks from the plaza, where they off-saddled the horses and mule and turned them into a pen with a wooden trough full of water. The water was piped to the pen from the nearby Rio Grande. To make sure their animals were fed, they forked hay over the fence themselves. They had to pay for two days in advance for five animals.

"Oh, well," Sammy allowed, "we'll get our money back tomorrow."

"I hope she knows how to sell gold. I sure don't."

On foot now, looking for a hotel, Sammy said, "I've learned something else about this part of the world: the wood houses are hotter than the hinges of hell this time of year, but the adobe houses are pretty cool."

Lighthorse, in a joking mood, said, "You white eyes could learn from us Injuns and the Mescans. We learned how to live here a few generations ago."

Matching his grin, Sammy said, "You're right about that. But I wonder—if it wasn't for us white soldiers—who would have conquered who, the Mescans or the Injuns?"

"It's whom, not who. You was sent to school and bought books and you still spell tater with a p."

"Oh, excuse me all to pieces, professor Lighthorse. I apologize profusely if I violated the long-standing, sophisticated, traditional rules of the King's English." Chuckling, Sammy said, "How's that for imitating a goddam West Point officer?"

"All right, all right, how about that one over there, the adobe house with the Plaza Hotel sign?"

"If it suits you at all, it'll seem like a palace to me."

Thick adobe walls kept the room cool, but that was all that could be said for it. The furnishings were a double bed, a scarred dresser with one drawer missing, a round mirror on a wall and a clothes tree. The one thing of beauty it held was a brightly patterned, hand-crocheted coverlet on the bed.

"Some Mexican woman did herself proud on that," Sammy commented.

Lighthorse sat on the bed, bounced a couple of times, and allowed, "Better than sleeping on the ground."

They washed their faces the best they could with lukewarm water in a tin pan. Then they went back to the Coronado Hotel and knocked on Mrs. Wilcox's door.

"Who is it?"

Sammy answered through the door, "It's us. We wondered if you'd like to take supper with us?"

Her voice was somewhat muffled, coming through the door. "Thank you very much, but I'm so weary I think I'll skip dinner tonight."

"All right. We'll be at the Plaza Hotel if you need us."

Their supper was beefsteak, mashed potatoes and gravy, topped off with peach pie. Then back onto the street.

"Listen, pardner," Lighthorse said, "I know it's against the law to sell liquor to Indians, so I reckon I'll go on back to the room and finish that book I started to read a couple of weeks ago. If you want to hoist a few, go ahead."

"What ain't good enough for you would taste like horse piss to me."

In the morning, the woman met them outside her hotel room door. "I've had breakfast, thank you. But listen, the bank won't open for two hours, so I would appreciate it if, in the meantime, you could find a buyer for my two horses and saddles. I'll pay you a ten percent commission."

"Oh, sure. You won't need 'em anymore."

The livery barn was the most likely place to start. But the hostler, an overweight Anglo in baggy bib overalls with a blue polka dot bandana hanging out of a hip pocket, shook his head. "Not offhand, but I do a little trading myself. Which two are you talkin' about."

They showed him the two horses, now happily munching hay in the pen.

The hostler scratched his stubbled face. "There is a feller that raises calves over west on the San Jose that said about a month ago he needed a couple more hosses, but he's prob'ly bought some already. Now if you want a fast sale, I'll give thirty bucks a head for 'em and, oh, say, twenty-five for the ridin' saddle and ten for the pack outfit."

"Thanks, but we'll ask around."

"Fine and dandy. If I buy 'em, I'll have to feed 'em hay 'til I can sell 'em, and I have to make a profit, you know."

"Sure."

Sitting in the plaza was interesting—for a while. Sammy always liked watching civilians going about their businesses and trying to guess what their businesses were. Lighthorse always liked watching white people going about their businesses and wondering how they lived and what they did for a living.

But after hours of that, they decided to find out how the woman was doing. "She should have sold her gold by now," Sammy mused. But when she answered their knock on her hotel room door, she shook her head. After inviting them to step inside, she explained:

"The bank doesn't buy gold. However, I did learn the name of a broker who does, and I have entrusted him with the box of nuggets and dust. He is going to have it assayed, then pay me accordingly."

"Assayed?" Sammy asked, standing with his thumbs hooked inside his cartridge belt. "Somehow I thought we were carrying the pure stuff."

"Oh, no. Henry and I separated the gold from the worthless minerals the best we could using primitive methods, but of course we couldn't do a thorough job. However, we think—thought—it's at least seventy-five percent gold."

"Oh. How long will it take to assay it?"

"Two to three days. I'm sorry. I know you'd like to

go on with your plans, whatever they are, but I can't pay you until I'm paid."

Sammy looked at Lighthorse. Lighthorse said, "Well, I reckon there's nothing to do but wait around."

Waiting in the plaza was beginning to get boring. Then a gent in rancher's clothes stepped up. "You the fellers that want to sell them two old ponies over at the livery?"

"Yeah," Sammy said.

"My name is Walt Tillsdale. I already looked 'em over, and I'll give a hundred and sixty for the whole outfit."

"You've seen 'em?"

"Yeah. Old Newt pointed 'em out to me."

Sammy and Lighthorse looked at each other. Lighthorse shrugged. Sammy said, "Well, that's probably as good an offer as we'll get."

"Only thing is," Tillsdale said, "I drove a buckboard to town and I've got a broncy team. You'll have to bring 'em out to my ranch in the mornin'. It's about twelve miles west on the San Jose. I'll pay cash money."

"I guess we can do that."

"Good 'nuff. I'll stay close to the house 'til noon." He told the two young men how to find his place, and said, "See you *mañana.*"

"We probably should have done some dickering," Sammy said, "but I never sold a horse before."

"Me either. When we bought ours we should have tried to talk down the price, but we didn't. We just ain't wise to these things."

In the evening, they again knocked on the woman's hotel room door, told her about their agreement with Walt Tillsdale, and asked if she wanted to have supper with them. "Thanks," she said, "but I have promised to have dinner with the gold broker." Fine. They said they'd leave early in the morning and be back by late afternoon.

When they got back, she wasn't there.

"She paid for two more days," the round-faced proprietor said. "I tink she vent out, but I didn't see her leaf."

"Oh. Well, we'll come back in the morning."

In the morning she still wasn't there. "I don't know vere she vent," the proprietor said. "Her bed vas not slept in last night."

Outside, Lighthorse said, "I don't know much about the ways of white folks, but this is . . . you don't think . . . she wouldn't . . ."

"Let's go check the stage office."

"Yep," the ticket agent said, scowling under his green eyeshade. "A woman who looked like that got on the Santa Fe stage first thing yesterday mornin', only she gave her name as Mrs. Hancock."

"Uh-huh," Sammy snorted.

Turning their steps back toward the plaza, he grumbled, "Goddam. I wouldn't have thought it. She seemed honest."

Lighthorse said nothing. They walked on a few steps, and Sammy remembered an old Chicago street saying. "Yep, partner. We've done been screwed, blued and tattooed."

Ten

Just to be sure, the partners went back to the Coronado Hotel late in the evening. Nope, no answer to their knock. The proprietor heard them knock and came out of his apartment. "I tink she has leff. Ven I didn't see her all day I looked in the room and there vas nodding dere but an empty pox with straps unt buckles on it. It iss von uf the poxes you emptied."

"Just like the one she put in your safe?"

"Chess, chust like dat von."

"I guess," Sammy said outside, "if we hadn't spent so much time in the army, if we'd associated more with civilians, we'd have got wise to her."

"She's a damned good actress."

"And we're damned big fools."

"If we went after her, we'd never catch her. The stage company has relay stations, and we ain't."

"Hell, if we did catch her, what would we do, stick a gun up her nose?"

"Might as well forget it."

After a moment of silence, Lighthorse said, "Well, we're not out anything but time."

"And we've got the hundred and sixty dollars for her horses and saddles."

"So we gained a little."

"That's better than nothing."

Sammy was still grumbling under his breath as they walked to the plaza and sat on a plank bench. There, he continued grumbling and swearing in a low voice, then suffered his depression in silence. Finally, Lighthorse said, "Well, what's done is done and what's gone is gone. What do you want to do now?"

Sighing, Sammy said, "Go on with what we were doing before we met that woman. I don't know of anything else to do."

Trying to be cheerful, Lighthorse grinned and said, "If that's what suits you, it tickles me to death."

"Yeah. That crazy German's mine won't be any harder to find now than it was a week ago. Let's go down the road this time where the traveling is easier. At least as far as Socorro."

"We could run into those robbers again, but now that the gold is locked up in somebody's safe, maybe they won't bother with us."

"We ain't got anything worth stealing, except two horses and a mule."

"Folks have been murdered for less than that."

"That's so. And if they see us, they ain't gonna be friendly."

"Well, what are we gonna do, quit the territory?"

"Naw. Let's go down the road to Socorro, then head southwest to the Pinos Altos. Stay off that desert between Socorro and El Paso. It ain't called the Jornada del Muerto for nothing."

Lighthorse said, "It's a two-day ride to Socorro. Let's start out early in the morning."

"Whatever suits you is fine and dandy with me."

* * *

They rode down a dry, dusty wagon road that par128alleled the Rio Grande to the small farming town of Belen. Green fields of vegetables, irrigated with water from the river and cultivated by big-hatted Mexicans with hoes, made an oasis of the town and its surroundings. The town, they discovered, was divided into a new section and an old section, with the usual plazas and a church. Their horses were fed in a feedlot managed by a Mexican who could speak only a little English, and the two travelers were fed in a Mexican cafe.

Stuffed with pork chops, frijoles and tortillas, they sat under a big cottonwood in the plaza and watched the people. Lighthorse commented, "There are more Spanish-speaking folks in these towns than Anglos. Maybe I should have learned Spanish instead of English."

"Most civilians in these parts can speak a little Spanish, and most Mexicans can speak a little English. We get along."

Well-fed and rested, their two bay horses and the gray mule were content to keep to a slow but steady trot the next day on the road to Socorro. The road was well-traveled, with light spring wagons pulled by two-horse teams, a string of freight wagons drawn by four-mule teams, Mexicans with small two-wheeled carts and burros and Mexicans on foot. The two young men reached Socorro by mid-afternoon.

Socorro was another farming village on the Rio Grande with another plaza and another adobe church. It was the last stop for travelers headed south onto the Jornada del Muerto, the Journey of Death, and the worst place to buy supplies.

When the *tendero* in the adobe mercantile told them the prices of everything, they wished they'd stocked up in Albuquerque. "Well hell," Sammy said, "we have to have provisions. I reckon we'll have to pay."

It was Lighthorse's turn to grumble. "We're being used again. This can get damned old."

"Yeah, this feller is getting rich off of travelers."

They loaded their pack panniers with tins of beef and ham, tins of vegetables, a stack of tortillas and a five-pound sack of coffee. They also bought two boxes of .44-40 cartridges which could be fired from their repeating rifles and their six-guns.

Carrying their panniers to the livery where they'd left their animals, Lighthorse quipped, "I didn't hire out to be a pack mule. If I had to do much of this, I'd start braying."

"We must have seventy-five pounds of grub here."

"We'll be up in those hills a long time. Unless we get lucky."

"Or tired of living that way."

"Or scalped by the Chiricahuas."

"Or run into another damsel in distress."

"Damned damsels can get out of their distresses themselves."

"Damned damsels is right."

The hostler slept in a small room at one end of the long barn, they were told, and their packs would be safe. They stacked the panniers beside their saddles and started walking back to the hotel they'd picked out. A short, stout gent in a gray hat, with his pant legs stuffed inside his high-top boots, spotted them from across the street, did a double take and stared. He had a pistol low on his right hip, and he had a star pinned to his shirt pocket. He angled across the street toward them.

"Well, I'll be damned," he said when he came closer. "Yessir, I'll just be double damned." Quickly he drew his six-gun and pointed it at the two. "This's my lucky day. I was wonderin' where I could find you two, and here you are, walkin' right to me."

Lighthorse and Sammy stopped suddenly at the sight of the gun. "What . . . ?" Sammy stammered. "What's going on?"

Smiling, Sheriff Elmer Pogue said, "Weel, I'll tell you what's goin' on. But first reach for the sky and turn around."

"But . . . why?"

The smile left the sheriff's face. "Do like I tell you and do it right now."

Glancing at each other, the two raised their hands and turned their backs to the sheriff. Pedestrians, both Anglos and Mexicans, stopped and stared. The guns were lifted from their buttoned-down flap holsters.

"I can see you two ain't gunslingers. It'd take you too long to get these hoglegs out of them army kind of cradles." He stuffed the guns inside his belt, holding them there with one hand. "All right now, march."

"March? March where?"

Lighthorse hadn't said a word.

"To the hoosegow, that's where. You two've got a lot of talkin' to do."

With curious townspeople watching slack-jawed, following a safe distance behind, the partners marched a block down the street, around a corner, down another street and around another corner. When they came to a flat-roofed adobe building, the sheriff said, "Right here."

The building had a sign over the door that read, "SHER-IFF—SOCORRO COUNTY."

Inside was a scarred oak desk with a bank of pigeon-holes on the wall over it, a spring-back chair, a gun rack holding two lever-action rifles and a double-barreled shotgun, and another straight-backed wooden chair. "Sit on the floor over there against the wall," Sheriff Pogue ordered. They sat next to a door with iron bars. The sher-iff settled his big rump into the spring-back chair.

"All right now. Ain't no use pretending ignorance. You know damned well why I'm puttin' you under arrest."

They knew now, but they said nothing.

"Me and my deputy had to take two pack mules and go get them two dead men you left up there in the Elk Mountains. What was left of 'em. Wasn't no fun, I'll tell you; and we couldn't identify 'em, and we had to bury 'em in graves with no names over 'em. You tell me, who was they?"

Sammy answered, "Robbers and killers. They fol-lowed us from Fort Bayard, and when they caught up with us we shot it out with 'em."

The spring chair creaked as the sheriff leaned back. "You say."

"Yessir, I say."

"Why didn't you tell me about that back there at Horse Springs?"

"We didn't want to stay around while you investi-gated."

Shifting his hard gaze to Lighthorse, Sheriff Pogue asked, "Don't you know nothin' about white folks' laws? Don't you know when you kill somebody you have to report it to the laws? Don't you know when you kill somebody you can't just ride off and leave 'em lay?"

Lighthorse answered with a drawl, "It's like Corporal—I mean Sammy—said. We wanted to get to Albuquerque."

"What'd you do with the woman?"

"Last we heard she was on the stage to Santa Fe on her way to St. Louis where she came from."

Sheriff Elmer Pogue kept his six-gun in his lap with his finger on the trigger as he stared hard at the two partners. Then he said, "You're in a lot of trouble no matter which way we cut it. Even if them dead men turn out to be thieves and murderers, you're in trouble for not reportin' a killin'."

"I hope you'll do some investigating."

"I already am. I sent my deputy down to Fort Bayard day before yesterday to see what he can find out, see if somebody can identify the deceased, and see where they come from. Where did that woman, that Mrs. Wilcox, come from?"

"She said she and her husband—her late husband—came from a town named Buckhorn, somewhere west of Kingston on the west side of the Black Range."

"You done told me some men killed her husband."

"That's right."

"Well, we'll find out. Meantime, I'm lockin' you two up. Pull off your boots."

Sitting on the floor, they pulled their boots off.

"Now your britches."

"Britches? Why?"

"I ain't takin' no chances on a hideout gun. Now do like I said. I've got a legal right to shoot you."

They had to stand up to take off their gunbelts and

pants, and they stood in their shirts and drawers while the sheriff searched their clothes. "All right, put 'em back on." Sheriff Pogue backed up to his chair and sat. When the partners were dressed again, he took a long key from a desk drawer, went to the door with iron bars and unlocked it. "In there."

It was a one-cell jail with no window, two iron bunks, each covered with a dirty blanket, and a bucket for a toilet. "Ain't the comforts of home," the sheriff said, "but jails ain't s'posed to be comfortable."

Sammy asked, "Aren't we entitled to a court-martial? I mean a trial? Or something?"

"When we find out exactly what happened, how the deceased got killed and all that, then we'll get the judge to set a date for a trial. Unless you plead guilty."

"How long will it take?"

"Who knows. You're gonna be here awhile."

Within an hour the partners were restless. Sammy paced the small cell and muttered. "We're the dumbest jackasses in the West. We should have told the sheriff about that engagement and the dead and wounded. That woman didn't just have to get to Albuquerque right away."

Lighthorse lay back on a bunk and said nothing.

"Goddammit, I guess I hoped the gunsels would come back for their dead, but I should have known better." He continued pacing. "Shit, all we did was defend ourselves. That can't be against the law."

Lighthorse resorted to something he'd begun learning at babyhood: Indian stoicism. And finally, Sammy sat on the other bunk and put his face in his hands.

Meals in the Socorro County jail were mostly beans and tortillas with small pieces of meat, sometimes pork and sometimes beef. It was always cold and barely edible. At first, Sammy only picked at his food, but Lighthorse ate every crumb. Then Sammy did the same. "They're feeding us whatever is left over from yesterday at one of the cafes, but it's food, and we have to stay strong."

Four days passed before they got any news, and the news was all bad.

Eleven

Sheriff Pogue stood before the cell, hands on wide hips, gray hat shoved back, revealing a high, white forehead. "You boys are in worse trouble than I thought."

Sammy looked up from his bunk and growled, "Why? How?"

"Well, sir," the sheriff seemed to be enjoying himself, "ever'thing you told me wasn't so." He paused, waiting for a reaction. Lighthorse said nothing. Sammy stood and came to the cell door. "What the hell are you talking about?"

"You said that woman and her husband worked a claim down at Buckhorn and that's where they got the gold."

"Yeah. Well?"

"Ain't so. They stole it."

"Huh?" Sammy gripped the iron bars until his knuckles were white. "What . . . ? That's . . ."

"Yup. My deputy got the whole story. He found two of the survivors of that gun battle up in the Elks, and what they said just don't match your story a-tall."

Even the impassive Lighthorse was sitting up now, listening.

"What," Sammy croaked, "did they say?"

"Well, sir, I'll tell you what they said. They said two gents robbed the Packrat Mine at a town named Buckhorn and he'ped theirselfs to a lot of gold dust and rich ore. The mine owner, man name of Harrels, didn't want to depend on what passes for the law down there and sent four of his own men after 'em. They could see, come daylight, that the thieves went horseback toward the Pinos Altos and there was three horses. They figgered there was two thieves packing the loot on a packhorse."

"Aw for . . ." Sammy shook his head, unbelieving.

"Yup. Well, they said they caught up with 'em in the Pinos Altos and there was some shootin'. They was just about to shoot 'em out of a gulch when you two come along and started blastin'."

Still shaking his head, Sammy protested, "Aw, godalmighty damn. We didn't shoot anybody, just drove 'em off."

"Well, what you done was you drove off the wrong side."

"Well, how in hell . . . goddammit, we were at Fort Bayard for three days. Why didn't they show up and tell their story there."

"They said they didn't know where you was 'til after you left. Then they got a couple more men and went after you."

Sammy glanced at Lighthorse. The Indian was staring at the sheriff but keeping his mouth shut. Still incredulous, Sammy said, "This is just . . . goddammit, I don't believe it. Why didn't they call out? Why didn't they holler and tell us who they were?"

"Said you didn't give 'em a chance. Said you shot two of 'em out of their saddles before they knew you was there. The dead men was Pete Hallman and Jacob Tenders. We'll have to make some tombstones now."

"Aw no." Sammy was shaking his head, frowning. "No, I don't believe it." He let go of the iron bars, turned his back on the sheriff, then faced him again. "Why didn't they pick up their dead?"

Sheriff Pogue lifted his hat, scratched his bald, white head, reset the hat. "I wondered about that myself. I reckon they was scared of your guns. And they had two wounded men to take care of."

"Well . . . goddam. We thought . . . aw hell. God-dammit."

Lighthorse finally spoke. "They threw a lot of lead at us, and they meant to kill us."

"What would you of done if you'd a been in their place?"

Sammy answered, "I sure would have hollered, said something."

"Well, you can tell your story to the prosecutor. He's the one that decides what crime to charge you with."

"The prosecutor?"

"Yeah, we got one. He's a farmer most of the time, but he knows somethin' about the law. He's been askin' about you two, and he's tickled to have somebody to prosecute."

"Aw, for crying in the street." Sammy turned, went to his bunk and sat with his face in his hands. The sheriff went to his desk and sat in the squeaky spring-back chair.

No one spoke for a long time. Sammy was so full of grief he couldn't speak. Lighthorse stared at the ceiling, his face expressionless. Eventually, Sammy looked at his partner with pain-filled eyes. "We're in a hell of a jack-pot, Lighthorse."

"Yeah." He answered without emotion, without look-ing at Sammy.

"That woman lied to us every step of the way. And we fell for it."

"Yeah."

"Now she's on her way to St. Louis a rich woman while we rot away in the guard house—jail."

"Unh."

Sammy walked to the cell door, then went back and stood over the Indian. "I'm going crazy in here. If I stay here much longer, I'll be a raving maniac."

The Indian's eyes shifted to his partner, and he spoke quietly, matter-of-factly. "We're gonna have to bust out of here."

No sooner did the sheriff leave his office than the two partners inspected every inch of the cell, floor to ceiling. The door was locked tight. The floor was two-inch lumber, the walls thick adobe. Even the ceiling was thick lumber, and the two guessed the roof was clay tile.

"If we had any kind of tool, we might work on that ceiling," Sammy said. "If we could cut through it, we could knock some of the tile off the roof."

"Too bad that law dog didn't let us keep our pocket knives."

"Not a tool of any kind. Say, maybe we could keep a spoon when they take away our supper dishes."

"Cutting through planks with a spoon would be slow work, but we've got plenty of time. That is, if nobody notices what we're doing."

When their suppers came, Sheriff Pogue did what he

always did; he ordered the prisoners to stand back against the far wall while the old Mexican carefully put their plates on the floor. The sheriff followed the same routine every time the cell door was opened.

Lighthorse kept his spoon, and the Mexican didn't notice.

But they had to wait until the sheriff went home for the night to start working on the ceiling. Working by the light of one candle, the only light in the jail, Sammy stood on tiptoe on one of the bunks and dug at a ceiling plank with the tip of the spoon. After a half hour he managed to tear one splinter loose. "I'm making progress."

"When you get tired I'll spell you."

"It'll only take a year or two."

Daylight arrived and they hadn't slept a minute, but that didn't worry them. They had nothing to do all day but sleep. What did worry them was they had only a foot-long scratch cut into the ceiling plank. Carefully, they hid the spoon and the splinters under a blanket while they waited for breakfast.

A day later they had a foot-long cut in the ceiling, and they guessed they'd break through it in another night. "But, shit," Sammy said, "it's gonna take forever to cut a hole big enough to crawl through."

Trying to make a joke, Lighthorse said, "Injun like snake. Crawl through anything."

"Sure, sure. What we need is some outside help."

They didn't get any help that day, but the next day they did.

It was a deputy who brought the little man, almost dragging him by the back of his shirt collar. The deputy, a wide-shouldered man with a trimmed brown beard,

ordered Sammy and Lighthorse back against the wall,
then unlocked the door with a key he took from a hip
pocket.

"In there, you little rat, and don't go makin' a fuss
or these two'll beat the shit out'n you."

The little man with a thin moustache and baggy wool
pants complained in a squeaky voice. "I told you before
and I'll tell you again, I didn't intend to steal anything.
I only meant to—"

"Yeah, yeah, I know. Hell, you had your hand in the
cash box and your fist full of money when the barkeep
caught you."

"But I didn't mean to—"

The deputy said disgustedly, "Shut yer yap."

The deputy shoved the key back into his hip pocket
and turned to leave. He stopped suddenly when the outside door opened. The man who came in was breathless,
like a man who'd been running. He gasped, "Dan'l, your
wife wants you to home. Your little boy's done broke
his arm."

"Damn," Dan'l grumbled. "If it ain't one thing it's
two or three." Without a backward glance he half-ran
through the outside door.

The little man turned away from the cell door and
looked over his cell mates. He was as small as a woman,
with long fingers and thin wrists. His shirt collar was
a size too big for his skinny neck. "You . . . you
wouldn't beat me up, would you?"

"Naw," Sammy said. "We ain't in the habit of beating
people up."

A weasel-like smile turned up the little man's mouth.
"That's good 'cuz I've got something you want."

"What?" Sammy asked, not really interested.

"This." The little man held up the key to the cell door.

"Huh?" Sammy saw it, but he wasn't sure he believed it. "How in the . . . how'd you get that?"

"He put it in his ass pocket and turned his back for a few seconds. That's all it took."

"Well, I'll be gone to hell."

"It takes a lot of practice, but I can steal a man's watch while I'm talking to him."

"You're a pickpocket?"

"Yessir, and a damned good one. It was just bad luck that I got caught today."

Lighthorse came to his feet and took the key from the little man's hand. He reached between the iron bars, bent his wrist and got the key in the lock. It turned. The door opened.

Whispering now, Sammy said, "Wonder where the sheriff is?"

"I heard he went up to Albukirk early this morning," the little man said. "He only has one deputy."

"We'll never get a better chance," Lighthorse said. "Let's go."

Twelve

They found their gunbelts, guns, money and folding knives in a desk drawer in the sheriff's office, then walked out onto the street in broad daylight. No one paid them any attention when they sauntered down the street as if they had every right to be there.

"Now, if we can just get our horses, we'll be on our way," Lighthorse said.

"Can't go anywhere without horses. Say," Sammy said to the little man, "where are you going from here?"

"If I can get a horse I'll head up to Albuquerque."

"Getting horses might be easy and it might be impossible."

When they approached the livery barn they knew it was going to be impossible. At least for the moment. The hostler was there, raking manure out of one of the stalls.

"He knows we're supposed to be in jail," Sammy said. "He'll holler his head off."

Looking at the sky, Lighthorse said, "Be noon soon. I hope he goes to one of the cafes for dinner."

"We'll have to stay out of sight 'til he does."

"Let's get over by the river, in them tall weeds, where we can watch 'im."

They crossed a road and squatted in the tall hogweeds and sunflowers along the Rio Grande. The little man sat on the ground beside them. "My name's Jason," he said. "What's yours?"

"Rather not say," Sammy answered. "I didn't want to know your name either."

"You gotta admit, you owe me something."

"Yeah, we do at that."

"Can you spare a few dollars? I'm broke flatter'n a fritter. That's why I took a chance in that saloon. I'm usually more careful than that."

Lighthorse took his roll of greenbacks from a shirt pocket and peeled off two fives. "Here. That'll keep you in grub for a while."

"Oh, oh," Sammy whispered, "there he goes."

Sure enough, the hostler was walking toward the plaza, wiping his face with a red bandana. The fugitives waited until he was out of sight, then hurried to the barn. Working fast, they caught and saddled their horses and loaded the pack mule.

"What about me?"

"Oh, yeah. I'll catch a horse for you; then we go in different directions, all right?"

Sammy found a saddle and bridle and put them on a sorrel horse that was standing in a box stall. The horse had white saddle marks on his withers and was not young.

"He ought to be gentle enough." To Lighthorse, Sammy said, "Let's get to hell out of here."

After leading their animals out the far end of the barn, they mounted and crossed the road again. They rode through weeds and cottonwoods until they were out of sight of the town, then got onto the road where their tracks mingled with dozens of others. Lighthorse looked back once to be sure the little man wasn't following them.

"We do owe him something, but if he's spotted and the deputy takes out after him, that'll give us a better start."

Not another human was in sight, and Sammy guessed it was dinner time for the whole town. "If we're lucky— I mean luckier—everybody will take a siesta after they eat."

"Just the same, let's get these ponies and this mule into a gallop."

With Lighthorse leading the mule and Sammy slapping it from behind with the ends of his bridle reins, they broke into a lope. After a few miles, Lighthorse said, "Here's a good place to cross."

The spot he picked wasn't the best crossing; but it wasn't too hard either, and it was a place that was seldom, if ever, used. River water covered their stirrups, and the animals had to climb a sloping cutbank on the other side. "A blind man could see somebody crossed here," Lighthorse said, "but there's nothing we can do about it."

"Maybe we can disappear in those mountains, the Magdalenas."

It didn't take long to reach the mountains, where the traveling was mostly uphill and downhill. They rode at a trot and a lope where they could, knowing they couldn't cover their tracks, but hoping to put the town of Socorro far behind them before the deputy got some help and came after them. There was no trail, so they kept their horses pointed southwest, careful not to get trapped in a dead-end canyon or under a steep ridge.

Every time they rode over a high point they stopped and studied their back trail. There was no one in sight behind them. At sundown they were more than halfway across the Magdalenas.

Their camp was cold and dry. They unsaddled their horses and the mule and hobbled them on good high country grass. "Got to keep 'em in good shape," Lighthorse said. "We sure need 'em." Supper was a tin of dried beef apiece and one can of beans. They ate quietly and listened. Just before dark they walked a mile back the way they'd come and looked for any sign of pursuers. They saw nothing. And before they rolled up in their blankets, they took another look.

"No camp fire anywhere. You don't reckon we got away clean?"

"Unh," Lighthorse grunted. "After all the bad luck we had it's time something went right."

"Just the same," Sammy said as they walked in the dark back to their camp, "we're fugitives from the law. I wonder how far we'll have to go to get plumb away. I wonder if we'll ever be able to go anywhere without always having to look back."

"Unh."

Shortly after first light they were riding again, picking the easiest routes, but trying to stay off the skyline. At noon they could see down onto the plains and across the plains to the end of the Elk Mountain Range.

"Which is better, Lighthorse, camp in the foothills tonight and get across the prairie as fast as we can tomorrow, or see how far we can get before dark?"

"I see a creek down there in that narrow valley. Let's water these animals and ourselves, then go down in the foothills, wait for dark, then get out on the prairie as far as we can before we have to stop for the night."

"You're right. I wish we could get across the prairie in the dark, but these horses need rest."

At the bottom of a talus slope, they dismounted, dropped their reins and let the horses graze without unsaddling. In another hour, the country was lighted by nothing more than a half-moon. On horseback again, they continued southwest at a steady trot until the horses began to tire. Then they off-saddled, hobbled the animals and sat on the ground and ate out of the hermetically sealed tin cans.

"They tell me," Lighthorse said, "you have to empty these cans pretty quick after you open 'em, or the contents will get tainted."

"Mine's empty already. Sooner or later we're gonna have to build a fire and fry that bacon. In fact, I haven't looked at it, but it's probably spoiled now."

Grinning in the dark, Lighthorse quipped, "Injun no need fire. Injun eat 'em raw."

"Injun get sick in the gut, too, and probably never know why."

"Injun got stomach like wolf. Never get sick."

"Huh-uh. Ain't so. Injun get the drizzling shits same like white man."

"White man sleep now. Injun watch, listen."

"They can't track us in the dark."

Keeping at a steady trot, posting in their saddles military style, they crossed the plains. By sundown they were near the bottom of the Elk Mountains, but their animals were tiring fast. All during the day, they'd repeatedly turned in their saddles and looked back. In the foothills, they stopped at a stream that came out of the mountains and let the animals drink their fill, then rode up into the short pines and scrub oaks and looked for a place to camp. Just before nightfall, they found a small grassy park.

After unsaddling, they walked back and looked back across the plains. "Unless they're riding in the dark, there's nobody close on our trail," Sammy said. "Let's see if that bacon is fit to eat. And make some coffee."

At mid-morning, as they were following a dim game trail on top of a pine-covered ridge, Lighthorse reined up and pointed at a mountainside across a narrow valley.

"See that? Ever see that before?"

"What?" Sammy asked, looking in the direction his partner was pointing.

"Indians call her the Lady Who Sees All, but white folks call her the Lady of Magdalena."

"Oh, I see her. I'll be damned. No, I've heard of her, but I've never seen her before."

What Lighthorse was pointing at was a rock outcropping with shrubs growing around it, which from a distance looked exactly like a giant woman's face.

"Boy, oh, boy," Sammy said. "Ain't that something." He shook his head in wonderment. "Yessir, that's something."

Traveling southwest, over ridges, through scrub oak, alder brush, and cedars, and then into the tall timber, they struck Beaver Creek a day later. The Pinos Altos Range was straight south. They still stopped on the other side of each rise to study their back trail, always expecting to see a deputy and a posse riding hard after them.

The blacktail deer were plentiful and so were the turkeys. On their way south, they saw four black bears, which were harmless. The New Mexico mountains were also home to the silvertip grizzlies, which were not harmless, but the travelers didn't meet any. Nor did they see any sign of anything human. They followed the creek where they could, but in places the stream ran through narrow gulches, which they had to go around.

It was while they were going around a narrow gulch that Lighthorse looked to the west, reined up and sat still a moment, thinking. "Know something, pardner, we're making a mistake following this creek. If there's anybody behind us, they know by now that all they have to do is follow the creek themselves, and they'll find us."

"You're right. What we need is a good rain to wash out our tracks."

"That might work, but it wouldn't stop an Indian tracker."

"Let's hope there ain't any Indians behind us."

Instead of staying along Beaver Creek, they turned to the southeast, riding through tall pines and spruce now. The white-trunked aspen grew in groves up here. Because of all the downed trees, the groves were something to avoid. "These trees grow fast and die fast," Lighthorse allowed. "Where there are quaking asp you'll never run out of firewood."

They came to a small creek that flowed down from the divide of the Black Range, and off-saddled.

"What we need is a good hard rain," Sammy said.

Looking to the west again, Lighthorse said, "We might get it. Not tonight, but tomorrow, soon after noon."

Lighthorse was right. White puffs of clouds began gathering on the western horizon the next morning, and by noon had joined other clouds. Soon after noon, the white clouds turned dark, and lightning flashed over west.

"It's coming closer," Sammy said, "the lightning. I can feel it in my hair. We ought to find a low spot where there ain't any tall trees."

"Yeah."

"But not in a gulch. She's gonna be a gully washer."

Lightning zigzagged too close for comfort, followed in two seconds by a crash of thunder. The partners dismounted, sat on the ground and prepared to wait it out. The storm was fierce but short. It started with tiny hailstones which quickly covered the ground like snow; then the hail turned to rain. Hard-driving rain. The horses and mule humped their backs and endured it. The two men had no choice but to sit on rocks with their knees up, arms wrapped around their knees.

Lightning split the sky. Thunder boomed like cannon fire. Then it was gone, moving east.

The two men were sopping wet when they stood and shook water off their hats. "Well"—Lighthorse grinned—"you wanted rain."

"Yep. Only problem is, the ground is wet now, and we'll leave tracks that nobody could miss."

"Maybe they'll think we're still following the creek and won't come across our tracks here."

"Well, let's get away from here and find a place to build a fire and dry out. It never rains in these mountains but it turns colder than a backyard privy in December."

The slab of bacon they'd bought in Socorro was thoroughly spoiled by now, so they had to throw it away and eat a meatless supper. Tossing a dead pine limb on the fire, Sammy said, "There's plenty of game, and we need some fresh meat; but I'm not sure I want to fire a gun. What we need is a bow and some arrows. That wouldn't make any noise."

"Injun kill meat. No noise."

"Sure, sure." Sammy grinned. "Most Indians don't hunt with bows and arrows anymore."

"Injun catch turkey. You see."

"Sure, sure."

Sammy didn't know how he did it, but true to his word Lighthorse caught a fat tom turkey the next evening. When they saw four turkeys come out of some alder brush, Lighthorse slipped off his horse, opened his folding knife, and went after them, walking softly.

Sammy kept quiet, watching. The turkeys turned and disappeared back into the brush. Lighthorse slid into the brush, too. In ten minutes he was back, carrying a freshly killed tom.

Grinning, Sammy said, "That do beat all. How did you do it?"

"It's an art," Lighthorse said. "Pick a place to camp, and I'll pluck 'im and dress 'im out."

"I wouldn't have believed it if I hadn't seen it."

Streams were everywhere following the rain, and they off-saddled near the edge of a pine forest where late afternoon sunlight slanted between the trees. While they were doing that Lighthorse talked, and Sammy learned more about Indians.

Thirteen

"Wanta know why Indians are better hunters than white men?" Lighthorse asked.

The thick forest behind them had a strong, pleasant smell of pine pitch. In front of them was a two-acre grassy meadow with wildflowers of all colors growing through tall grass. Aspen leaves trembled on the other side of the meadow.

"Why?"

"Because we've always had to hunt to live. And up until a few years ago we had to do our hunting with bows and arrows and lances. Some Indians still do. We had to get close."

"Uh-huh." Sammy was listening, interested.

Lighthorse unbuckled one of the heavy canvas panniers, took out the coffeepot and coffee, straightened his back and faced his partner. "We started learning to track and stalk as soon as we learned to walk. When we were little kids we played stalking games. We grew up learning."

"Yeah, I can believe that. But there are a few white men who can track as well as an Indian."

"Right. But only a few. Every Indian is a good tracker and stalker."

"That's why General Cook said it takes an Indian to catch an Indian."

"That's why the army hires Indian scouts." Lighthorse located a cloth bag of salt, picked up the dead turkey and went to the stream.

Not only were the Indians good hunters; Lighthorse plucked and dressed the turkey faster than Sammy could get a hot fire going. With good grass for grazing and fresh, clear water, the partners had a good camp. Turkey roasted on green aspen sticks was delicious. They put out the fire as soon as the cooking was done and the coffee had boiled, and ate in the dark.

"We've been lucky." Sammy leaned back on his elbows. "The sheriff was out of the county, the deputy had a sick boy to take care of, and we had a pickpocket for a cell mate. It even rained when we wanted it to. But you know what? I keep expecting somebody to yell 'Hands up,' and turn around and find myself looking at a badge and a gun barrel."

"Me, too," Lighthorse said. "I'll never feel safe. I've been worrying about it, wondering what to do. I don't like being wanted by the law, living in fear of being recognized and locked up again, but I don't know what to do about it. I could head for the reservation, let my hair grow and hide among the other Indians, but I don't want to live that way either."

"If we had enough money, we could hire a lawyer and demand a jury trial. A smart lawyer could tell our side of it."

"Wonder how much it would take?"

"Whatever it takes, we ain't got it."

"We need to find that crazy man's diggings."

"Well, that's what we started out to do about ten years ago."

Chuckling in the dark, Lighthorse said, "Seems that long, all right."

Lying on one end of a tarp with the other end folded back over him, a duffle bag for a pillow, Lighthorse listened to the breeze whisper through the pine tops, listened to their animals graze, looked at the stars that seemed so close he could gather a handful, and let his mind wander.

He recalled the day he first met the young trooper named Corporal Samual Collins.

It happened because of the longtime war between the Muache Utes and the Jicarilla Apaches. The Utes blamed the Apaches, and Lighthorse believed it was so. Every young buck in the Apache camps wanted to be a war hero, and the Apaches were always raiding the Ute camps, stealing horses, taking prisoners. The favorite recreation in the Apache camps was torturing prisoners of war.

But now and then the Utes took the war to the Apaches.

Lighthorse was eighteen, tall, lithe and strong when a dozen young bucks raided an Apache camp in the Jawbone Mountains. They fired their guns and arrows and stole the camp's horse herd. The Apaches fought back. Three of the Utes—Lighthorse and two older men—were captured.

The other two were wounded and not able to run. Lighthorse's pony was shot from under him. They were tied to posts set in the middle of the Apache camp and left there the rest of the night and all the next day. Tied so tightly the bonds nearly cut off blood circulation.

One of the older men slumped over, held up only by his bonds. Lighthorse and the other managed to stand up straight. During the day, children taunted them and threw rocks at them.

After dark, the Apaches gathered around a big fire, their black eyes glittering in the firelight. Then the fun started.

The weakest one was first. They stripped him naked and tried to force him to stand straight. He was too weak from a bullet wound in the stomach. An old squaw, wrinkled, gray hair stringing down her back, pulled a long-bladed knife from somewhere in her deer-skin clothes and cut his penis off. The man's head came up and he grimaced, but made no sound. Within seconds he slumped again.

A burning stick was taken from the fire and shoved between his legs up to his crotch. His head came up again, and his teeth were bared in pain. That got some grunts of satisfaction from the gathering. But it wasn't enough. Burning sticks were shoved under his armpits, and in his hair. He cried out. The gathering laughed. Then he slumped again.

The Apaches jabbered in their language, pointed at him. An older man, wearing a necklace of human teeth taken from the bodies of war dead, walked up to the Ute and cut his throat. The head fell forward as blood ran down his body. The old Apache smeared the blood of the dying man on his own body. Laughter came from the gathering.

Because he was the youngest and strongest, Lighthorse was last. The second Ute had died a hideous death, cut to pieces, skin peeled from his chest. His screams had brought howls of laughter from the Apaches.

The teenage Ute was determined not to scream. He didn't want to give the enemy the pleasure of hearing him scream. They cut his clothes off; then the old man cut a gash across his stomach. Lighthorse managed to hold back any sound at all. Another gash was cut across his chest. Gritting his teeth, the young brave stared hatred at the Apaches. Then came the real test. The Indians seemed to be having a contest to see who could strip the biggest piece of skin from their victims.

A younger Apache, wearing only moccasins and a breechclout, chest painted with a weird design, took a knife from his belt and approached, grinning a cruel grin. Then the gathering started jabbering, and another buck came forward, scolding the younger one. Lighthorse believed they were arguing over whose turn it was. They argued while the gathering jabbered. The old man stood and faced the crowd, talking and waving his arms. Slowly, a few at a time, the Apaches stood and walked away. The two dead Utes were cut from their posts and carried off. Lighthorse was left alone.

They'd be back. If not tomorrow, tomorrow night.

Lighthorse's wounds bled during the night, but not enough to send him into shock. He lost consciousness and slumped against his bonds. By morning his hands were numb, and he believed gangrene had set in. They might as well kill him. He only hoped he could die without giving them any entertainment.

For the next twenty hours he slipped into and out of consciousness. When he was conscious, kids taunted him, threw rocks at him and beat him with sticks. An old squaw jabbered at him in the Apache language. She grinned a toothless grin. Lighthorse guessed that what she was saying was he could be revived before the torture began again. He would feel the pain.

Then everything changed. A young buck came riding into camp on a horse that was running as fast as it could run and had run as far as it could run. He yelled and screamed. Men ran toward their horse herd, carrying rifles and pistols. Women worked fast, bundling belongings and shouldering them. The camp was being evacuated.

A gunshot was fired. More shots. The Apaches were running, scattering.

Lighthorse watched through a semiconscious haze, not understanding what was happening. Still more shots. Then rapid gunfire. Horses galloped through the camp. Horses ridden by white soldiers. Someone was behind him, cutting his bonds. He fell in a heap. He tried to get up, but got only to his hands and knees before he collapsed again. A man's hands straightened him out on his back. A white man's face hovered over him. The white man rubbed his wrists and hands, rubbed hard, desperately. When the blood flowed into his hands it felt like a thousand hot needles were being stuck into them. With the pain, life returned to his hands. His fingers twitched. The white man's face smiled, said something in the white man's language, and poured water from a canteen into his mouth. Lighthorse was barely able to swallow.

The young Ute was only vaguely aware of being carried and lifted into a wagon. At times he could feel the wagon's jolts as it bounced over a roadless ground, but most of the time he felt nothing. He thought he was only imagining a white man sitting beside him. Once, he was conscious enough to raise his head and ask where he was, but the white man didn't understand. The white man said something in a soothing voice. Blackness closed in on Lighthorse.

He didn't know how long he rode in the wagon. He didn't know where he was when he was lifted out and carried inside some kind of hogan. Through a haze he saw men bending over him, talking. White bandages soon covered his chest and stomach, and the young soldier was holding his head up and trying to force something into his mouth. Whatever it was, it tasted good, and Lighthorse swallowed. The young soldier smiled.

He was in the sick tent a week. Other sick men lay on cots on either side of him. Some groaned and some cried. Lighthorse kept quiet. Every day the young soldier came to see him. As soon as Lighthorse could understand what was going on around him, the soldier pointed to himself and said, "Corporal Collins." Lighthorse didn't understand.

Then another Indian was brought in, a Ute, wearing white man's pants and a vest. His black hair hung down to his waist. He said he was paid by the soldiers to help them hunt Apaches. He said he hated the Apaches and considered it a pleasure to help find them. The Ute scout taught Lighthorse a few words in the white man's language: food, water, toilet. Lighthorse asked him how to say thank you, and he practiced until he could say it himself. Corporal Collins taught him more words in English, and laughed with him when he tried to pronounce those words.

When he was strong enough, Lighthorse lived in a part of the fort that was reserved for Indian scouts. He learned more English and within a few weeks was able to communicate with the white men. Corporal Collins came often to visit, and one day pointed at himself and said, "Friend." He pointed at Lighthorse and said, "Friend." Both young men smiled. When Corporal Collins held out his right hand, the Indian didn't know what he was supposed to do until the soldier took his right hand, grasped it and shook it, then pointed to himself again and said, "Friend." He smiled from ear to ear when Lighthorse pointed at himself and said, "Friend."

That was when the young Ute decided he, too, wanted to scout for the soldiers, and wanted to learn the white man's ways. He and Corporal Collins were the best of friends in garrison and in battle.

Fort Union had a school for the officers' children, and the teacher, a middle-aged, bearded man from an eastern city, seemed to enjoy teaching Indians. Lighthorse was even allowed to attend some of the classes. The children ranged in age from six to sixteen. They laughed at the Indian's attempts at speaking English. At first he was embarrassed, but he soon learned that if he laughed with them, they slapped his back and shook his hand. He learned to read and write English.

Troopers kidded him about his skin color and long hair. They called him names such as redskin and blanket ass because of the way the scouts liked to wrap blankets around themselves. But they smiled when they did that, and he realized they were only joshing. He smiled, too, and had his hair cut the white man's way. He became a "Civilized Indian."

Now, as he lay on his back and stared at the stars, he fingered the scars on his stomach and chest and worried about the future. He had no idea what the future held for him, but right now it sure didn't look good.

Fourteen

Making tracks straight south now, the partners stopped at a creek that they believed to be the middle fork of Negrito Creek. There they camped and tried to figure out which way to go the next morning.

Sammy said, "That crazy German—Schlotman, was his name—said something about walking across a prairie, and he thought he was going north. I don't know anything about a prairie in these parts, do you?"

Lighthorse was squatting next to a fire and finishing the remains of the roasted turkey. "Everywhere I've been in these mountains you've been. I don't know 'em any better than you do."

Chuckling, Sammy said, "What we need is an Apache scout. The Apaches know this country."

Lighthorse grunted, "Sure. And he'd lead you right straight to Victorio or Naiche, Cochise's son."

"The way I heard it, Cochise died at peace with us white men, but his son didn't like being transferred to another reservation over in Arizona somewhere, and went on the warpath."

"I heard the same thing."

"Well, if there is a prairie and we keep heading south, we'll come to it. If we don't . . ." Sammy shrugged.

"If we don't, we'd better keep going south, all the way to Mexico. If I could learn Spanish, maybe I could pass for a Mexican."

"Some Mexicans have as much Indian blood in them as Spanish, but, naw, you'd never learn to talk Mexican without an accent."

"I can't even go back to the army now that I'm a wanted man."

"If you were rich, your ancestry wouldn't matter."

"Yeah, sure."

Sammy knew his partner was feeling glum, and he wanted to say something that would make him feel better. There was nothing he could say, so he said nothing.

Between the middle fork and the west fork of Negrito Creek, they rode through a small park where elk antlers lay at the foot of nearly every tree. "This is one of those places," Lighthorse said, "where the bulls come to get away from the cows during the moulting season. Here's where they rub off their old horns and scratch the velvet off the new ones."

"Yeah, I can see the bark rubbed off all the trees."

At Negrito Creek, where the creek came out of a canyon, they off-saddled and hobbled their horses and mule and had started to make camp when Lighthorse suddenly stopped dead still and listened. Sammy stood perfectly still, too, wondering what his partner was listening for. Then the Indian said calmly, "Pardner, I think we're in for it."

"What? Apaches or white deputies?"

"See that cliff over there at the end of the canyon? We'd better pile up some rocks and get ready for a fight. I've never heard a turkey gobble this time of year."

"What's a turkey gobble got to do with . . ." And suddenly Sammy knew.

Working fast, they picked a spot under a shale cliff with a slight overhang, and began carrying rocks to build a fortress. They worked furiously until they had a semicircle of rocks high enough that they could lie out of sight behind it. Then they carried their panniers inside the half circle, ate a cold supper and waited.

When it turned dark and nothing happened, Sammy whispered, "Maybe we're mistaken."

"No."

And when they heard the whippoorwill calls and coyote barks, they knew for sure.

"We can only hope there ain't too many and they don't have guns," Sammy whispered.

"They ain't attacked yet, and that's a pretty good sign they're waiting for help. If we're lucky, help won't come."

More whippoorwill calls. A coyote yapped to their left and was answered by another coyote.

"Better get some sleep," Lighthorse said. "If they come, they'll come at first light. I'll stay awake."

"If we can't fight 'em off, save one bullet for yourself."

With a dry chuckle, Lighthorse said, "You don't have to tell me that."

The night was dimly illuminated by a half-moon, but shadows under a line of trees seventy-five feet in front of them were black. Within two hours after dark the moon was high enough to light up one side of the canyon to the west. Moonlight didn't touch the other side of the canyon, and it, too, was black. The two men waited, straining their eyes, trying to see into the dark places.

They'd done this before, waiting with a squad of soldiers for daybreak, knowing the Apaches would attack, not knowing whether they would survive or be killed. They'd learned to be patient, wait for a target.

Lighthorse whispered, "They'll steal our animals."

"Yeah. We're in a pickle no matter what."

Waiting, Sammy lay on his back, his hat for a pillow, and closed his eyes. Lighthorse would stay awake. Lighthorse would hear everything, and he'd wake up his partner when the time came. But Sammy couldn't sleep. He tried to figure out what they'd do if they survived. Plan ahead. Always plan ahead. That was impossible. First they had to stay alive.

Daylight came slowly, first illuminating the tops of the pines, then slowly lighting up the ground. The partners had their eyes to the peepholes they had left in their low rock wall. Not an Indian was in sight.

"They're out there," Lighthorse whispered. "You can bet on that."

"They are for a fact."

They heard a swish and a thud, and a long lance appeared in the ground near Sammy's left shoulder. Two eagle feathers were tied to the shaft. Glancing up to the top of the cliff, they saw a lone Indian looking down at them.

"Damn," Sammy muttered, "that's close."

"Move over here under the overhang. I don't think he can reach us over here." They shifted positions, moving more to their right. Another lance suddenly appeared in the ground right where Sammy had been. "I'd sure like to get a shot at that son of a bitch."

"Duck," Lighthorse said.

They pulled their heads down just as a flock of arrows whistled past their fortress and clacked into the cliff behind them. Looking through their portholes, they saw the attack coming. Both men raised up and fired over the top of the wall, levered and fired rapidly. Four Indians fell. The others stopped, looked at one another, then backed into the pines. Gunsmoke was a haze between the partners and the Indians.

Sammy whispered, "If their only weapons are arrows, we've got a chance."

"They didn't know about these repeating rifles."

"If they've fought the army, they probably thought we had single-shot breech loaders."

"Don't count your lucky stars yet."

A rifle cracked from under the trees, and a slug went splat against a rock next to Sammy's porthole.

"That sounded like an army carbine," Lighthorse said. "No doubt took it off a dead trooper."

"Boy, they'd sure like to kill us and get these guns."

"Here they come again."

The Apaches were in a skirmish line now, shooting arrows, yelling and screaming like crazy men. Their rifle cracked, but the slug buried itself in the cliff. Another Indian held a six-shooter, shooting wildly. The partners had to show themselves to shoot back, but being disciplined soldiers they made their shots count. Indians fell.

An arrow nicked Lighthorse's left shoulder. He didn't even notice. When Sammy saw the pistol aimed at him he instinctively ducked, then reminded himself he had to keep shooting. He aimed and fired, and the savage with the six-shooter fell.

A loud, long war whoop came from one of them, and the Indians stopped their advance. Then they began backing off again. Soon they disappeared into the forest.

Reloading as fast as he could make his fingers work, Lighthorse said, "They're wondering if it's worth it."

Sammy rolled onto his back to reload and glanced at the top of the cliff behind them. "Look up there. Smoke signals. They're sending for reinforcements."

"They'll probably get some. But maybe their signals will draw a detail of troopers, too."

"Whatta you think? Will they attack again?"

"Not until reinforcements come."

"Then they'll swarm all over us."

Grimly, Lighthorse said simply, "Yeah."

"You're bleeding. Your shoulder. Is it bad?"

Lighthorse ran his hand inside his shirt and fingered the wound. "Naw."

Time passed. Sammy opened a can of tomatoes, and both men ate out of the can, spearing the vegetables with their pocket knives. They drank sparingly out of their canteens.

"Know what I'm thinking?" Lighthorse asked.

"I can guess 'cause I'm thinking the same thing."

"We're fools for waiting here. We should have tried to escape in the dark last night."

"Which way did they come from?"

"South."

"Then, if there was any more where they came from, they'd all be here by now."

"Right."

"So, if we could get past 'em in the dark, we might get away without running into any more of 'em."

"Right."

"One thing's sure, if we stay here long enough, we're gonna be easy pickings."

"Yeah."

Fifteen

It was a long wait. They ate canned pork and a can of beans. Another lance thunked into the ground, but it missed them by two feet. Sammy said, "Apaches like mule meat. Wonder if they'll butcher our mule."

"Probably."

The rifle cracked from over in the woods, and the lead slug ricocheted off the rock wall and smacked into the cliff. Sammy saw the puff of smoke and fired his repeating rifle at it. He had no way of knowing whether he'd hit anyone.

"That Apache can't shoot too good. I guess he ain't got enough ammunition to practice."

"Some of 'em can shoot. We know that."

"Yeah, we've seen more troopers killed by bullets than arrows."

"Speaking of arrows, look what's coming."

The Apaches were shooting arrows from the cover of pines, aiming high, hoping they'd come down inside the rock fortress. Most fell short, but a few did fall inside. The partners saw the missiles coming and dodged.

"Hurry up darkness," Sammy muttered.

Small white clouds were drifting under the sun, creating spots of shade. "We'd better eat while we can,"

Lighthorse said. "Eat the canned stuff. That's harder to carry."

They opened tins of beef and fruit and ate. "What we leave behind will feed some of them savages," Sammy mused. "We can't carry much."

Working on his hands and knees, keeping a watch around them, Lighthorse picked the lightest of the groceries from the panniers and put it in a burlap bag. They allowed themselves another drink from their canteens.

Finally, the sun slid behind a high ridge to the west. Its light reflected off low clouds, turning them several shades of red and purple. The colors changed slowly as the sun sank lower beyond the horizon. Then it was dark.

"Time to go," Lighthorse whispered. "Before the moon comes up."

Slowly, carefully, they crawled over their barricade and worked their way into the canyon, carrying their rifles and the sack of groceries, staying on the darkest side. More night bird calls and coyote barks came from behind them. As always, Lighthorse led the way, groping with his fingers, careful where he put each foot down. In places they had to wade in the creek, getting their feet sopping wet, but that was the least of their worries. They stopped long enough to hastily fill their canteens, then went on.

When they came to a fork in the canyon, they didn't know which way to go. Either way could lead to a dead-end trap. Lighthorse hesitated only a few seconds, then took the right fork. Gradually, the half-moon rose, casting a dim light on the far side of the canyon. The two men hugged the cliff on their side.

Step by step they went on, not talking, but stopping

now and then to listen. The catcalls were farther behind them now. Lighthorse stopped, studied the far wall a moment, then strained his eyes to see up the dark side. He whispered, "I think we can climb out here. We'd better get out while we can. Come daylight we could be trapped in here."

"I'm right behind you."

It was slow going, hand over hand. Their biggest fear was they'd loosen some dirt or rocks which would slide and clatter to the canyon floor. Each step up was a careful one. They stopped every thirty seconds to listen.

Lighthorse said, "I can see some stars. We're getting there."

"I don't hear those birds and coyotes anymore."

"Wait 'til daylight. Then you'll hear 'em."

They knew when they no longer had to step up that they were on top of the canyon, but that's all they knew. The dim moonlight showed a line of black shadows ahead, and they guessed that was a forest. They headed for it. Under the lodgepole pines and spruce, they stopped, sat on the ground and hugged their knees.

"First it was wait for daylight, then it was wait for night, and now it's wait for daylight again. We're spending a lot of time waiting."

"It's harder to wait than it is to do something," Lighthorse said. "But I don't think we're wasting time."

"Me, I'd like to get as far away from those blood-hungry savages as we can."

"We might want to go back later, see if there's anything left of our stuff."

"Go back?"

"Sure. The Apaches ain't gonna stick around long."

Sammy lay back on a layer of pine needles, using his hat for a pillow. "Wake me up if anything happens."

He eventually dozed. Lighthorse sat cross-legged on the ground, wide awake even though he hadn't slept for two nights. Shortly before daylight Sammy turned onto his side, then suddenly remembered where he was. He whispered, "Lighthorse, you there?"

"I'm here."

"I'll keep watch. You sleep."

"Naw. Be daylight soon."

They hugged their knees and waited. Again.

As before, the sun lit up the treetops first, and the partners discovered they were on the edge of a vast forest of pine, spruce and aspen. Only a few short alder bushes grew between them and the canyon.

With the daylight came the faraway whoops, yells and screams. "They can see we're gone," Sammy said, "and they ain't happy about it."

"The question is will they come after us."

"Even I could track us up here. We'd better quit the country."

"Not yet. We can get over there where we came up and wait for 'em. If they try to climb out of the canyon where we climbed out, we can take potshots at 'em."

"Yeah. We can hit a few of 'em before they get wise and go around."

That's what they did. And they didn't have long to wait. Even before the sun was over the horizon, the Indians came, running up the canyon, stopping where the man signs led up the sloping canyon wall. The two ex-soldiers waited until four Apaches were climbing hand over hand, then raised up and opened fire. The four slid down to the canyon floor and lay still. The others turned and ran back the way they'd come.

"How many did you see?" Sammy asked.

"Ten or twelve. Enough to make dog meat out of us if they catch us in the open."

"Well," Sammy drawled with a half grin, "would you agree that now is the time to make tracks?"

"Yeah, but let's go back in the direction we came from."

"If they come around the defile, we'll run right into 'em."

"Canyon, Corporal, and I'm guessing they'll go west out of there, thinking that's the way we'll go."

"You know 'em better than I do."

"Besides, I wanta go back to our camp, see if there's anything left."

"Whatever suits you tickles me pink."

They backed away from the canyon edge and hurried back into the woods. From there they walked east, staying under the trees where they wouldn't be easy to see, stepping over downed timber, but paralleling the canyon. When they came upon the stumps of pine trees, they knew white men had been there ahead of them and had built a cabin. But the stumps were old, the tops weathered gray, full of ants. Then they saw the cabin, what was left of it.

It sat in the middle of a small clearing. The roof had caved in. The door was gone, and the two windows were gaping holes. "Oooh, boy," Lighthorse said, pointing. "I'll bet those are human bones over there."

For a good five minutes, the partners stayed under cover of the trees, their eyes searching. Nothing human was in sight. Little striped chipmunks scampered around the cabin, and a long-eared squirrel scolded them from a limb over their heads, its tail jerking every time it chirped. Two ravens flapped overhead and lit on the top of a tall spruce. They sat there a moment, then flapped away.

The men stood still, ready to run back into the woods at the first sign of an Apache. The ravens came back and were joined by two others. They sat near the top of a pine across the clearing, and cawed and croaked.

"Does that mean anything?" Sammy whispered.

"Naw. Those birds talk all the time, but they don't always tell us anything."

"Well, if we're gonna have to fight Apaches again, that cabin would make a good fort."

"Right. Let's go over. But run. The faster we get there the better."

Run, they did, and they didn't stop until they were in front of the empty doorway. There, they took a long, careful look around. The bones were scattered, but a human skull lay nearby with grass growing through the mouth and eye sockets.

"Killed by Apaches, no doubt," Sammy said.

Nodding toward a rusty axe on the ground, Lighthorse said, "Caught 'im chopping firewood."

Inside the cabin, the fallen roof covered the furnishings and most of the floor. A pack rat's nest, made of twigs and grass, nestled in a far corner. Stepping over debris, the two men went to the windows and looked across the clearing. Lighthorse made his way over pieces of rotted roofing poles to the other side of the room, where he peered between two logs of the wall, a place where the mud chinks had fallen out.

"Whatta you think?" Sammy asked.

"Let's wait here awhile. Eat what we've got. If the Apaches come this way looking for us, they'll show up soon."

"And if they don't show up soon, they're not coming, huh?"

"That's my guess, but it's only a guess."

"Well, let's see what we've got to eat."

"A few cold flapjacks left over from yesterday morning and some dried apples. That'll keep us from starving."

Eating, keeping watch, Sammy said, "I b'lieve we killed at least ten Apaches."

"Killed or wounded. Either way, that many are out of the fight."

"They say in the army it's better to wound some of the enemy than to kill 'em. If you wound 'em, others will have to take care of 'em."

"Makes sense."

After they ate, Lighthorse found enough bare dirt floor to lie down. While he slept, Sammy kept watch, crossing the room often to look between wall logs. Mid-afternoon they decided the Apaches had given up on them and had traveled on.

As they left the cabin, Sammy wondered aloud whether they should bury what they could find of the human skeleton. The rib cage was about forty feet from the skull with grass growing between the ribs. Arm and leg bones were scattered farther. Sammy picked up a dried and curled leather shoe and, hearing something rattle, turned it upside down. Foot bones fell out.

Lighthorse said, "We ain't got a shovel, and if we gathered up what we could find of 'im and piled rocks on 'im, we'd be here 'til dark. We can't stay here that long."

The rocky ground went downhill from the cabin, and the partners walked parallel to the canyon until they came to where the ground leveled and the canyon ended. "Over yonder is the creek where we first forted up," Lighthorse said. "Let's go over and see if anything is left."

Nothing moved ahead of them as they walked to their campsite. No horses, no mule. Inside their half circle of rocks they found their panniers ripped apart and four piles of human feces.

Sammy grunted, "What they didn't want they shit on."

"Well," Lighthorse sighed, "that means they're not coming back."

"I don't think I want to stay here either."

"It'll be dark pretty soon. The Apaches didn't go after us like we thought they would. They went downstream, horseback. Let's sleep downstream somewhere and figure out what to do next."

Lighthorse picked up a skillet and the coffeepot, decided they hadn't been ruined. He walked into the pines and back, walking slowly, studying the ground. "I hoped to find a bow and some arrows, but they picked everything up."

Sammy commented, "It has to be a lot of work, making arrows and arrowheads. Especially with what tools they've got."

The partners' blankets and bed tarps were gone, and their bed that night was nothing more than a grassy spot beside Negrito Creek. In spite of that they slept—until about one o'clock. Sammy woke up cold, and had to get up and walk around to get his blood circulating fast enough to warm his body. Lighthorse woke up, asked what was going on, then went back to sleep. In the morning, Lighthorse had reached a decision.

"I'm not trying to get shut of you, pardner, but I've got a chore to do alone."

"What? Why alone?" Sammy was eating a handful of dried apples.

"Like I said before, nobody can track and stalk like an Indian. I'm gonna go after our horses, and I can do it better by myself."

Sammy stopped chewing long enough to give that some thought, then resumed chewing. "Yeah, you're right. They'd hear me coming from a mile away. But do you think you can find 'em and steal our horses back?"

"I've done things like that before."

"I'll wait here, then. Are you sure you're coming back?"

"Yep. If I'm alive and can travel, I'll be back."

Sixteen

Sammy didn't expect to see his partner again that day or night or maybe even the next day. He stayed under the trees most of the time, but did go back to their half circle of rocks to search again for anything salvageable. Under the remains of a pannier he found two tins of sardines to make his dinner out of. He considered boiling some of the dried fruit in the coffeepot, but was afraid to build a fire. More Apaches could be coming from the west, or the ones they'd fought might be only a few miles away. Most of the time he sat on the ground under the pines and worried.

The dried fruit was getting damned old. If he had Lighthorse's skills, he might catch one of the cottontail rabbits or a squirrel. He tried throwing rocks at them, but missed every time. Shooting them could bring back any Apaches that might be within hearing distance, and sounds carried a long way in the high altitude air. Too, he couldn't eat raw meat.

He waited and worried.

How long should he stay around? And what would he do if Lighthorse never came back? He counted his money and discovered he had enough to buy another horse and saddle. That is if he could find an old saddle for sale. He could also get some bread and jerky. If Lighthorse didn't come back, he'd walk until he came to a settlement of some kind. Then what?

He was wanted by the law, and if arrested, he could be charged with murder. He could be hung. The thing to do, he decided, was to get far away, out of the territory. Arizona, maybe. Find a way to earn some money and make his way to California.

One thing he didn't intend to do was to wander around these mountains by himself. He could end up like the man whose bones were scattered near that cabin.

By the end of the second day he decided he'd start out in the morning, follow the creek and see where it led. There had to be a settlement somewhere down there.

When daylight came he was ready. It didn't take much to get ready: pull on his cold, damp boots, tuck his shirttail in, shift his six-gun to his left side, butt forward, stuff his pockets with dried fruit. Walk. He ate while he walked. And he hoped he'd meet Lighthorse coming back.

Following the creek downhill was easy most of the way, but there were places where he had to climb over small boulders or go around the big ones. Just before noon, he saw where the Apaches had turned away from the creek and headed in a northeasterly direction. Deciding which way to go took some thought. If he wanted to try to find his partner, he should follow the Apaches. If he wanted to find a settlement, he should follow the creek. Another thought popped into his mind. What if Lighthorse made it back to where they'd parted? Would he wait and hope Sammy came back, too?

Lighthorse wouldn't wait long. What he'd do was he'd

track Sammy down. Lighthorse could do that. Sammy followed the creek.

At mid-afternoon he saw the settlement.

It wasn't much. From where he stood, on the side of a brushy hill, Sammy saw where the creek poured out of a narrow gulch and wound its way through the settlement. He could see what looked like a mercantile built of pine logs, and a saloon. A dozen or so log cabins and clapboard shacks were scattered on either side of the creek. Up on the side of a hill to the west was a long, rambling building with smoke coming out of a smokestack. Three smaller buildings squatted near it. Only a few people were in sight. All men. Two saddle horses were tied to a hitch rail in front of what looked to be a saloon. A light wagon with a spring seat and two horses hitched to it stood near the saddle horses.

Half-sliding, Sammy made his way down the hill to the wagon tracks that passed for a road into town. Two men standing, talking on the street, looked him over as he walked, but nobody spoke. His eyes took in everything, hoping to find a cafe. He saw none. What he did see caused him to stop abruptly.

The two horses tied in front of the saloon were both bays, one with a snipe nose and the other with black legs. Both were saddled. A gunnysack about a third full hung from the saddle horn of the darker bay, and full saddlebags were tied behind the saddle of the other. Blanket rolls were tied behind both cantles.

Their horses. His and Lighthorse's.

Where was Lighthorse? Not in the saloon. It was illegal to sell liquor to Indians. Not in the mercantile. From the looks of the gunnysack and the saddlebags,

Sammy guessed Lighthorse had already been in the mercantile. Where?

Thinking he'd ask someone, Sammy walked through the wide-open door of the saloon. The place was crowded. Men lined the bar and surrounded a table back against the far wall. Suddenly a cold fear turned Sammy's guts into one big knot. The fear ran up his back and settled in his throat.

Lighthorse was seated at the table, a hangman's noose around his throat and his hands tied behind his back.

Their eyes met, but Lighthorse showed no recognition at all. His face was without expression of any kind.

"What—what's going on?" Sammy asked of a short, stocky man standing near him.

"We're fixin' to hang us a Injun."

Words were sticking in Sammy's throat. "W-why. What did he do?"

"Do?" The man's squinty eyes looked Sammy up and down. "Hell, he's a Injun."

"He-he doesn't look like an Indian."

"Oh, he's tryin' to look and act like a white man, but anybody can see he's a goddam redskin."

"Well, when are you gonna hang 'im? And where?"

"Purty soon. Say, you're a stranger in these parts, ain't you?"

"Yes, I'm just traveling through."

"Where'd you come from and where you headed?"

Instead of answering, Sammy asked, "Where is the hanging gonna take place?"

"East of town a ways. There's a big ol' pine over east that's got a big limb just right for hangin'. Where'd you come from, Silver City?"

"Yeah." Sammy turned and went outside.

For a long moment, he stood in the street beside the tied horses and tried to think of a way to rescue his partner. He couldn't shoot it out. Even if he could cut Lighthorse's bonds and hand him a gun, they couldn't shoot their way out. Fifteen or twenty men were inside the saloon, all of them armed.

Then an idea popped into Sammy's mind. It wasn't much of an idea, but maybe . . . if they were lucky. . . .

Moving fast now, he untied their two horses from the hitch rail and checked the cinches. He mounted his horse and led the other, going east, expecting to hear someone raise a racket, holler "Horse thief," or something. But the street was nearly deserted, with only a woman in a poke bonnet coming out of the mercantile. The men were in the saloon, sopping up booze and anticipating an execution. Having fun.

As he rode past the last shack, Sammy booted the horses into a run. He galloped past the big ponderosa that he guessed was the hanging tree and kept going for about two miles. He followed the wagon road past a curve around a line of buck brush, and when he came to a brushy draw off to his left, he turned up the draw and pushed through the scrub cedar until he was out of sight of the road. There, he tied the horses to the limbs of a cedar bush and pushed his way back, leaving his rifle in a saddle boot.

On the road again, he ran back the way he'd come, holding his six-gun down against his left side as he ran. "Gotta run," he said under his breath. "Can't be too late."

He slowed to a walk when he got past the first shack and saw the light wagon coming, pulled by the two-horse team. Lighthorse sat in the back of the wagon, the hangman's noose still around his neck. His hands were still tied behind his back. One man was on the backless board seat, handling the driving lines. A mob of men followed the wagon on foot. The mob was laughing, drinking whiskey out of bottles and having a good time.

Sammy walked alongside the wagon, trying to look like one of the mob. Lighthorse saw him, but again showed no recognition, just sat in the low bed of the wagon without expression. Sammy glanced around him, licked his lips for courage, then quickly climbed into the wagon.

A man yelled, "Hey. Hey there." But Sammy was behind the driver, wrapping his left arm around his throat. At the same time he yelled at the team. "Hit up. Hit up there." He dragged the driver backward off the seat, then threw him over his left hip onto the ground. The driver landed heavily, barely missed by a rear wheel. The team was trotting now. While Sammy grabbed for the lines, two of the mob tried to climb into the wagon box. Lighthorse jumped to his feet and kicked them in the face. They fell back.

With the lines in his hands, Sammy yelled at the horses, whipped them on the rump with the end of one line, urging them into a gallop. The mob was running after them, yelling, cursing. Another man got his hands on the tailgate. Lighthorse stomped on his fingers. The man let go.

"Hit up. Heeyup," Sammy yelled. He got the horses into a wild stampeding run. The mob was left behind. A shot was fired. Lighthorse dropped to his knees and pulled his head down. A bullet punched a splintery hole in the tailgate of the wagon box. Another whistled over Sammy's head.

"Hi, horses. Hi."

The wagon rattled down the tracks, bouncing over rocks. The two horses were running flat out now. Bullets splintered the tailgate, spanged off the iron-tired wheels. Sammy turned in the seat, drew his six-gun and fired two rapid shots.

Then they were out of six-gun range, and then they were around the scrub oak, out of sight of the mob.

"Get ready to jump," Sammy yelled.

Lighthorse stood, staggering to keep his balance in the bouncing wagon. "I'm ready."

"When I holler, jump."

Sammy tied the lines to the brake handle, leaving them slack. He yelled, "Hi. Hi. Hi. Heeyup."

They were approaching the brushy draw. "All right, pardner. Get ready. Jump."

Lighthorse jumped, hit the ground on his feet, but fell hard and rolled, trailing a long rope with one end tied in a hangman's noose around his neck. Sammy jumped, landed on his feet, but lost his balance and slid on his stomach, skinning his hands and one cheek. Immediately, both men jumped up.

"In here," Sammy said, digging his folding knife out of a pants pocket. He ducked into the brush with Lighthorse right behind him. They stopped long enough for Sammy to cut his partner's bonds. Lighthorse loosened the noose around his neck and lifted it off over his head. His hat fell off. He picked it up, clamped it back on his head, picked up the two lengths of rope and tossed them under an oak bush.

"The horses are up here," Sammy said. "Let's make tracks."

Mounted, they rode at a gallop, tearing through the scrubs, ignoring the dozens of tiny scratches, a torn shirtsleeve, urging their horses on. Lighthorse carried the gunnysack on the saddle in front of him, ducking his head to let his hat brim protect his face. At the end of the gulch, they rode out of the scrubs onto a grassy slope, kept their horses running uphill. Sammy reined sharply to his right and headed for some scattered cedars. His partner followed. Finally, on top of the slope, they reined up and looked back. No one was in sight behind them.

While the horses' sides heaved and their nostrils flared, Sammy grinned at Lighthorse. Lighthorse grinned at Sammy. Neither could think of anything to say for a long moment. Then, still grinning, Lighthorse drawled:

"Well, another day at the office."

Seventeen

Riding west, uphill into the higher elevations, Lighthorse Jones said to his partner, "If those blood-thirsty sons of bitches are smart, if they've got any sense at all, they'll forget about us and get ready for an attack from the Apaches. I tried to warn 'em. I told 'em about a big bunch of Chiricahuas gathering east and north of 'em, and they ain't gathering there for a picnic. And most of 'em have got rifles."

"Well, they were warned, then. If they're too damned stupid to heed the warning, there's nothing we can do about it."

Their horses were climbing steadily, going around boulders as big as houses, staying in sight of Negrito Creek. Only scrub cedars and buck brush grew here, but tall timber was ahead of them.

"I feel sorry for the women and kids, if there are any kids, but the goddam men can go to hell."

"If they'd tried to hang me, I'd feel the same way. In fact, I feel that way anyhow."

"I asked in the general store what the settlement was called, and guess what, it's Buckhorn. That's where that woman, that Mrs. Wilcox, said she and her husband came from."

"That big building up on the hill and the little shacks around it must be the mine they were supposed to have robbed."

"It's a stamp mill. Gold is being taken out of some mines around there."

"If the warning goes out, then, there ought to be enough men in the town to fight off the Apaches."

By now it was night and dark. Black dark. Lighthorse said, "Be a full moon pretty soon."

"Right now I couldn't find my ass with both hands. We'd better stop and wait for the moon. Don't want to wander off in the wrong direction."

"Yeah."

They dismounted and sat on the ground, hanging on to their bridle reins. The horses, with their good night vision, cropped the grass around them.

"Let's go back to where we camped last and figure out which way to go from there," Lighthorse suggested.

"Suits me. How did you do it? Steal our horses back."

"Barefoot, most of the time. About this time of night, when it was the darkest."

"Didn't they have a guard?"

"Yeah, but he's dead."

"Oh." Sammy didn't need to hear about how the guard died. Lighthorse talked on.

"I watched 'im from dusk 'til after dark, and by the time the night turned black I had our horses located. And our saddles. And I was right behind 'im."

"I'll be damned."

"They had their saddles piled between me and where their horses were grazing. I picked out our saddles by feel and carried 'em under some trees, but then I had to wait for the moon to catch these two horses. I didn't have to go barefoot after that. I figured the horses were making enough noise that my footsteps wouldn't draw any attention. Of course, I didn't stand up straight and walk right to 'em, and I didn't lead 'em right straight to the saddles."

"And nobody came to check on the guard or anything?"

"Yeah, but after I left. I heard 'em yell, and I heard a ruckus, but I was gone."

Chuckling, Sammy said, "Only an Indian could have done that."

"I saw the town down there while I was tracking the renegades, and I figured I'd go warn 'em and buy some provisions."

"The Apaches know it was an Indian who stole these horses, but they'll take it out on the white folks anyhow."

"Some white folks somewhere."

"Maybe they're going to Mexico. Old Victorio likes the Mexican mountains."

"He likes to raid on the U.S. side, then run back to Mexico where the army won't go after 'im."

"Did you hear about those Cheyennes in eastern Colorado who left the reservation and attacked wagon trains and murdered settlers and ran back to the reservation where they figured nobody would bother 'em?"

"Yeah. The way I heard it a bunch of volunteers from Denver and eastern Colorado got fed up and took the war to the enemy, reservation or no reservation. Killed a hell of a bunch of Cheyennes."

Shaking his head in the dark, Sammy said, "Too bad it has to be this way."

"Unh."

* * *

By the light of a full moon, the partners found their old campsite easily. After doing some searching and deciding there were no fresh signs of Apaches, they hobbled their horses and made a meal of cured bacon, beans and bread. And coffee. Stomachs full, they put out the fire and talked in the dark.

"I think everybody is convinced," said Sammy, "that old Schlotman's diggin's are somewhere in the Mogollons. I wish I could have heard him tell about it, but I reckon he didn't make much sense."

"No, they say he was out of his head. Plumb crazy."

"But rich. Or he would have been if he'd lived and could find his way back."

"I've heard a lot of talk about the nuggets he had in his haversack, and a lot of troopers have said they're gonna go looking for his diggings when their enlistments are up; but as far as I know nobody has done it."

"I think we're the first."

"He said something about crossing a plains, but he was too far south to have been on the San Agustin Plains. He said he got lost in the Pinos Altos, and wandered down onto some plains, then followed a creek into some mountains."

Sammy snorted, "Huh. What we're doing is trying to follow an old trail described by a crazy man."

"That's so, and if I had anything better to do, I wouldn't be doing it."

Shortly after sunup they were riding south, picking the easiest route around the canyons and ridges. Lighthorse caught and killed another turkey, which they had for supper. Sammy noticed he had a new skinning knife, and commented on it.

"You thought of everything. Without that hatchet you bought we'd have a hell of a time gathering firewood, and that knife is something we've been needing. These pocket knives are too little."

"I bought supplies 'til I believed I had all our horses could carry. And 'til I ran out of money. Besides"— Lighthorse glanced at his partner—"I don't want to cut our meat with the same knife that cut an Apache's throat."

Sammy grinned. "That would be sort of unsanitary."

"I've got to find a sandstone to sharpen this one on. The store edges won't do."

There was no way around the long, high ridge south of them the next morning, and they had no choice but to go over it. They made a half-dozen switchbacks, riding around boulders and through tall pines, before they reached the top. "Aw, goddammit," Sammy grumbled. "You get over one ridge and damned if there ain't another." They were looking down on a sagebrush valley and across it to another long, high mountain.

Pointing, Lighthorse said, "See those two bucks down there. That one with the narrow rack would be mighty good eating."

"Think you can get close enough? And risk a shot?"

Lighthorse dismounted. "Stay here and hold the horses. We need some meat." He took his rifle and started walking and sliding downhill. Sammy watched him until he disappeared in the sagebrush. The two deer continued grazing on the grass that grew between the bushes. A shot, and one deer went down on its knees, then fell over on its side. The other buck bounded away. Lighthorse stood up and waved.

Sammy didn't ride straight down off the ridge, but made more switchbacks, letting his horse pick their way. By the time he was down in the sage, Lighthorse had the carcass on its back and was cutting the best part of it off the hindquarters.

"We'll eat for a while," he said.

They carried the meat across the valley to where a natural spring seeped up through the ground and ran downhill to the east. While Lighthorse cut the meat into meal-sized pieces, Sammy climbed up the south side of the ridge and broke dead branches off a lodgepole pine. When they had a hot fire going, they dropped the meat into the hot coals, and inhaled the smell of roasting venison.

Sammy commented, "Cooking the Indian way, we don't need a skillet or pot or anything."

"Injun not need pot. Injun not ever see pot 'til white man come."

"Sure, sure, but I noticed you used plenty of white man's salt."

"Eat 'em without salt if have to."

"Yeah, sure, uh-huh."

The roasts were burned on the outside, but tasty. They cut off slices with Lighthorse's knife and ate with their fingers. Chewing, Sammy asked, "Did you Utes ever have a toothache?"

"Unh."

"What did you do about it?"

"Injun tie bad tooth to horse's tail. Tell horse 'Scat.' "

Laughing around a mouthful, Sammy said, "It's a wonder you didn't get your heads yanked off."

"Sure got rid of bad tooth."

It took half the next morning to get to the top of the ridge. From there they looked down on a sagebrush and yucca prairie with a creek meandering through it. To get to it they had to push through a mile of thick scrub oak, so thick they got down and led their horses, bending low and pushing with their arms.

"They say," Sammy mused aloud, "that cowboys think it's a disgrace to walk and lead a horse. They say cowboys won't go where a horse can't take 'em."

"Cowboys don't feel natural on foot. They believe if the Creator wanted men to walk, he would have given us four legs."

Sammy chuckled. "Cowboys wouldn't like the U.S. cavalry."

They wondered, when they came to the creek, if it was the Duck Creek they'd heard about. "I don't see any ducks," Lighthorse said, "but this looks the way I've heard it described."

"If it is, it comes out of the Mogollons, and we can follow it upstream and start searching the canyons."

Their supper was more of the roast venison, supplemented with a corn tortilla apiece. Then as usual they doused the fire and sat in the light of a full moon. Sammy asked, "What all did you hear about Crazy Schlotman and his diggin's?"

Lighthorse leaned back on his elbows, legs straight, and began: "What I heard was a detail from Bayard went up into the Pinos Altos to cut some firewood and bring back some fresh meat. They had about a dozen troopers led by Sergeant Mulhanny, a wagon pulled by two mules, and a German cook.

"They chopped firewood 'til they had a wagon load,

then went hunting. The cook was Schlotman, and he wanted to hunt. Sergeant Mulhanny wanted him to stay in camp; but Schlotman kept asking to be allowed to go hunting, and finally the sergeant gave his permission."

Lighthorse turned over onto his left side, and continued, "Well, old Schlotman took a carbine and left. That was the last anybody saw of him for about four weeks. When Sergeant Mulhanny and some of the privates went looking for him, they found a trail of blood. They followed the trail to where a deer lay dead. What they figured was old Schlotman had shot and wounded the deer, then tried to follow it to where it lay down and died. That was how he got lost. They were gonna search for him 'til they found 'im, but they were attacked by a bunch of Chiricahuas. Sergeant Mulhanny took an arrow in the throat and died. Four other troopers were shot through with arrows before they beat off the attack. The rest of 'em believed they were damned lucky to get back to the fort alive.

"Four or five weeks later old Schlotman came staggering back to Bayard looking like death about to happen. His shoes were worn out, and his feet were damn near bare. His shirt and pants were torn, his hair was long and he had a beard that had never seen a comb. He was within a couple of inches from dying of starvation.

"But he held on to that haversack.

"When they asked him where he'd been they got nothing but a lot of crazy talk. Somebody managed to open the haversack and saw it was about a quarter full of very high grade ore. In fact, the way I heard it, it was almost pure gold.

"Well, of course everybody wanted to know where he found it. I think he tried to tell 'em; but his mind wasn't working right, and he didn't make much sense.

"He lived a few days, then died."

Sammy lay on his back with his hands under his head and finished the story. "Everybody figured he'd accidentally stumbled on a vein that anybody would recognize as gold. Even a pair of dummies like us. And we figure if he found it by accident, we can find it by looking for it."

"That's what I figure."

"I think we're going in the right direction. He said something about a prairie with a creek running through it, and the creek is supposed to come out of some mountains." Sammy was beginning to feel excited. "That's where we are now."

"Well now," Lighthorse drawled, "don't go counting your nuggets yet. In this territory, all creeks come out of the mountains."

"Just the same, pardner, I've got this feeling. I've got a feeling we're gonna find gold and we're gonna make a pile of money."

Chuckling, Lighthorse said, "Let's just hope the piles we get don't need surgery."

Eighteen

It was as Lighthorse had said, all creeks in this territory came out of the mountains, and this one was no exception. By noon the partners found themselves on the talus slopes of a range of mountains that they believed were the Mogollons. They stopped where the creek poured down a steep canyon. The only semblance of a trail was an old, dim game trail that paralleled the creek out of the canyon.

"That trail was made by deer and elk," Lighthorse said. "They can go places horses can't."

"But a man on foot might go up there, and Schlotman was on foot."

"I'll hold the horses if you wanta go have a look."

While Lighthorse held the reins of both horses, Sammy walked into the mouth of the canyon, and soon felt swallowed up by it. The day was a sunny one, but the sun didn't shine in here. The game trail came down from a canyon wall that was so nearly vertical no horse could climb it. In fact, as Sammy looked up at it he could see where a rock slide some time in the past few years had wiped out most of it. Climbing over fractured rocks and pushing through thick brush, he followed the stream to a waterfall about five feet high. Clear water splashed happily into a pool below the fall, crashed against boulders and went on out of the canyon. Beyond the fall was more thick brush and boulders.

"Hell, a rabbit couldn't get through here," Sammy muttered to himself. He stood there a moment, looking up at the cliffs and more granite boulders that looked to be hanging onto the sides of the cliffs. A bullet could knock them loose and send them falling into the creek, he surmised. Kind of spooky in here. He turned and headed back to the sunlight.

Lighthorse looked at the sky, and allowed, "When the sun is straight up like it is now, a feller could get turned around and not know which direction is which. If Schlotman didn't go up that canyon, he went somewhere else. Let's ride along here and see if we can pick up another game trail."

Turning their horses east, they rode along the talus slopes until they came to a dim trail that led up a high hill that was steep, but not so steep a horse couldn't climb it. Still, twice before they reached the top, they got down and led their horses past sheer dropoffs, knowing that one little shift in the saddle could cause a horse to take a misstep and fall fifty feet or more.

At the top, standing among a scattering of short pines, Sammy sighed with relief and took a deep breath. Lighthorse grinned a weak grin. "Yeah, I was sort of holding my breath, too."

"If old Schlotman climbed that, he must have been convinced he was going in the right direction."

"He knew he was gonna have to climb some hills to get back to Bayard."

They rode along the top of a ridge until it sloped down into a narrow valley of buck brush. There was nothing to do but follow another game trail down into the valley, but instead of pushing through the brush, they rode alongside it, uphill from it, climbing around boulders in places.

Sammy commented, "I can see how a man could get lost. These valleys look too much alike." He repeatedly turned in his saddle to see what the country looked like behind them in case they came back this way. When they came to a rocky gulch that went uphill from the valley, they reined up.

"This is a gulch," Sammy said.

"Yep. It's the real genuine thing."

"Nobody has found gold on top of a hill."

"Nope. Only in the gulches. So I've heard."

"So?"

Lighthorse stepped down. "So, let's go take a look."

Walking, stepping around rocks and tufts of wheatgrass, they looked. They looked for any sign of digging. They looked for quartz rocks. They looked for any man sign. The gulch led them uphill to the top of a bald knob. There, they turned and walked down the opposite side of the gulch.

Back at their hobbled horses, Sammy said, "Oh, well, this is only one gulch. Hell, there are a million gulches, valleys and canyons in these mountains."

"Yep, only nine hundred and ninety-nine thousand to go."

"Make that nine hundred, ninety-nine thousand and ninety-nine."

"Unh. Injun count to a thousand. Injun quit counting."

"That's not the way I heard it. I heard Indians don't count."

"All Injuns count. All but one. Lost two fingers in fight with Jicarillas. Count no more."

Chuckling, shaking his head, Sammy said, "Well, when you count a thousand defiles, I'll be ready to quit."

"Gulches, Corporal."

The coming night forced them to quit for the day. They found a small stream that had been a bigger one earlier in the year, and built a fire. Roast venison and potatoes baked in the hot ashes made up their supper. With only two blankets apiece, Sammy woke up cold in the middle of the night. He stood, walked around in a circle in his bare feet, then lay down again, muttering to himself, "I'll be glad when the sun comes up and warms things up."

The sun didn't come up. Clouds had moved in during the night, and thick fog swirled around them. So thick it took them twenty minutes to find their horses. Thick, damp, cold fog. A fire of cut buck brush kept them warm—until they got wet. Before noon, a drizzling rain began. There was no shelter of any kind in the valley, not even a tree to get under.

Without saying anything Lighthorse picked up the hatchet and walked away into the fog. Sammy believed he was going somewhere to empty his bowels and cut more firewood. But eventually, after hearing chopping noises, he went to investigate. Lighthorse was cutting buck brush and stacking it in a pile. "Planning on a bigger fire?" Sammy asked.

"Make 'em shelter. Injun shelter."

"I thought about that, but without trees how can you make a shelter?"

"Watch. Learn from Injun."

Sammy watched, and when Lighthorse gathered an armload of cut brush, he picked up the remainder and followed him. The Indian had found a granite boulder, about shoulder high, that had rolled down from the mountain slope hundreds, maybe thousands, of years earlier. In front of the boulder, Lighthorse had two scrub oak sticks standing tied to each end of a six-foot-long horizontal stick. Two longer sticks were tied to the ends of the horizontal stick to form a frame for a lean-to.

"Bring the saddle blankets," he said. "Bring everything."

While Sammy carried their saddles, blankets and supplies to the lean-to, Lighthorse cut leafy tops off the buck brush and carried it by the armload to the boulder. Next, he took the two saddle blankets and stretched them across the leaning sticks, then piled the scrub oak tops across them to make a roof. "Water will drip through all this," he said, "but we won't get as wet under here as we will out in the open."

"You're right. And if we can get a good fire going right here, it'll warm up that granite, and maybe we can get some heat from it."

It was better than no shelter at all, but water did drip through the oak boughs and saddle blankets, and the partners were still wet. Lighthorse took off all his clothes, sat on the ground naked and held his clothes close to the fire on a stick. The clothes steamed. Sammy did the same. Then they dressed and held their blankets close to the fire. Though a cold drizzle continued, the blankets were soon warm and only slightly damp. They rolled them into tight bundles and put them under the bottom of the boulder where the ground was dry. After that they could do nothing but sit under their shelter near the fire and hug their knees.

Lighthorse quipped, "Injun hide like horse hide, shed 'em rain. Horse like rain. Keep 'em flies off."

"I wondered why you ain't shaking with the cold like I am."

"Injun tough. Injun take cold baths from babyhood. Break 'em ice in winter to take cold baths. Make 'em tough so can stand cold."

Shaking his head, grinning in spite of chattering teeth, Sammy said, "That explains it. I guess."

They ate more of the venison roast, but believed it wasn't far from spoiling. After the venison it would be cured bacon, and when that spoiled it would be beef jerky. Lighthorse hadn't bought any of the hermetically sealed canned food, believing it was too heavy and awkward to carry on a saddle horse. They drank two pots of boiled coffee, trying to keep warm.

The night was miserable. Enough water dripped through their roof to keep them damp and cold—too cold to sleep—and they spent the night cutting buck brush and adding it to the fire. Morning was still foggy, but the rain had stopped. At mid-morning the sky lightened somewhat, which gave them hope that the weather would clear up.

By noon the sun had come out for brief intervals. "Don't say anything," Sammy warned. "You'll scare it away." The sun disappeared again. But now that the rain had stopped they were able to dry their clothes and blankets. Sometime during that night the stars came out, and by daylight only wisps of fog hung in the cedars. The partners broke camp in the early morning sun and rode up the valley to where it widened at the top of a low cedar-spotted hill.

Sammy said, "This sun feels so good I sorta hate to get under the trees again. But, well, which way?"

"Where would a man who was lost go? If the sun was out, he'd know which way was east, and unless he was out of his mind he'd know the fort is east."

"Let's go east."

The partners spent two weeks wandering in the Mogollon Range, searching canyons, arroyos, gulches and narrow valleys. They saw no sign of anything human. Three times they were caught in mountain thunderstorms, and they spent three more nights wet and cold. When they came to the mouth of a canyon with a stream running out of it they decided to stay there long enough to build a shelter.

This time they built their lean-to under a big ponderosa, and they cut and stacked enough aspen trunks to make a reflector. They built their fire between the reflector and their lean-to.

"If we get any more of that lightning, I'm getting away from this tree," Sammy said.

"Lightning strikes mostly in the daytime up here, and we're gonna be busy looking for gold in the daytime. And getting rich."

Feeling better now that he was warm, Sammy said, "Damn betcha."

About five hundred feet uphill, the canyon widened onto a ten-acre meadow. Small beaver ponds were strung across the meadow like beads. The remains of a cabin sat near the creek.

Walking to the cabin, Sammy said, "We don't need another skeleton."

There was no skeleton. Most of the roof was still intact, but the one door had fallen off its leather hinges. All they found inside was a table made of aspen trunks and split pine poles, one chair and a bunk against a far wall made of the same material.

"He left and took everything with him," Lighthorse said.

"There's no stove. He did his cooking outside."

"He was handy with an axe. He did a good job of splitting those pine trunks to make a flat tabletop."

"Well, we don't need that shelter we built down there now. This roof is better than anything we can build with a hatchet."

"I wouldn't bet on it. It probably leaks like a net bag."

"Well, whatta you say, let's bring the horses up here. There's better grazing and everything."

It was dark by the time they rode their horses up through the canyon, but they found plenty of dead pine limbs to build a fire. After smelling the venison, they carried it back into the woods and left it there for the coyotes and foxes. For supper they fried cured bacon.

They were lying by the fire, talking very little, when Sammy suddenly sat up. "What in hell is that?" He was pointing at two bright eyes just outside the light of the fire.

"A skunk," Lighthorse said. "It won't hurt you. Probably made its home inside the cabin."

It wasn't just one skunk; it was a black-and-white mother with three little ones tagging behind as it walked past the fire and through the cabin door. "As long as it keeps its tail down it's no threat," Lighthorse said.

"Well, so much for sleeping inside the cabin."

"She'll share it with us. Indians have made pets of skunks."

"Just the same, I'm giving her plenty of room."

After a moment of silence, Sammy said, "You don't think that whoever built this cabin was a prospector, do you? If he was, he must have found something interesting or he wouldn't have stayed here long enough to build a cabin."

Lighthorse grunted. "No, he was a trapper. He trapped all the beaver out of the creek and left."

"Yeah, I noticed that all those beaver dams look old, and I didn't see any beaver." Sammy turned that over in his mind, then added, "And that means there's nothing around here that looks like gold. If there was, he'd have found it."

"Naw, there's nothing here. We'll have to keep moving."

With a dry chuckle, Sammy said, "We're gonna run out of canyons and gulches in another ten years."

"Yeah," Lighthorse drawled, "there can't be more than nine hundred and ninety thousand left."

Nineteen

In ten more days they were out of groceries and were living off the land. Lighthorse unraveled a length of grass rope and made rabbit snares and fish line out of one strand. Where he found a rabbit trail through the brush, he hung his snares and caught a few rabbits.

"I'll tell you something about rabbit meat," he said one night after eating a cottontail rabbit roasted over an open fire. "You can't live on it. I don't know why, but Indians learned long ago that if you try to live on rabbit meat, you'll die of the shits."

"You Indians learned from experience what medical scientists haven't figured out yet."

Fish, too, wasn't the best of foods. Lighthorse caught brown trout with a hook he'd made out of a piece of pine bough. He'd whittled the stick so it had sharp slivers on each side, then baited the slivers with whatever insects he could catch. "Fish," he said, "can keep you from starving, but it's not strong food. It won't keep you strong."

"We need some venison, but I haven't seen a buckskin for at least two weeks. Or a turkey or anything."

"I'll tell you what will keep you strong," Lighthorse said, kicking over a downed pine that had rotted. "This."

He showed his partner a few white grubs, then popped them into his mouth and chewed. "This keeps bears fat."

With a wry face, Sammy said, "I'll have to take your word for that."

Dandelions, which Lighthorse ate raw, but which Sammy preferred boiled, made up part of their diet, along with clover roots smoked over a fire.

When Sammy asked how he knew what wild vegetation was edible, the Indian answered, "From generations of experience. I'll tell you, though, pardner, if you don't know what you're eating, don't eat it. You can die of the shits quicker than you can starve to death."

But living off the land wasn't to their liking. Their clothes were ragged, and Sammy hadn't shaved since they'd run from Socorro, only trimmed his sand-colored beard as close as he could with a knife. His Indian partner didn't have a beard. And even Lighthorse admitted he was hungry for a beefsteak, mashed potatoes and gravy. While living with white folks he'd developed a taste for white man's food.

Just thinking of beefsteak, biscuits and sorghum, red beans and bacon made Sammy's mouth water and his stomach growl.

"It's decision time, pardner."

"Yep," Lighthorse agreed. "And it's an easy decision to make."

"Someday, somebody will find Crazy Schlotman's diggings, but not because he's looking for it. It will be pure luck."

"A lucky accident," Lighthorse agreed, and added, "We didn't really expect to find it, did we?"

"Naw. It was just something I wanted to try."

"I tried to make myself believe we'd find it, but in the back of my mind I didn't really expect to."

"Another decision: where do we go?"

"That's an easy one, too. I sure as hell ain't going back to Buckhorn, and I don't know as I'd be treated like royalty in any other settlement. That leaves Bayard."

"I've got enough money to buy some groceries at the sutler's. We can eat for a while."

"Got any plans beyond that?"

Sammy shook his head. "No. I'll worry about that later."

It took five days to ride to Fort Bayard, five days, five rabbits and one turkey. When the fort was finally sighted, the partners felt like cheering. But they reined up in surprise.

A small settlement had sprung up. It was only a handful of houses made of logs dragged down from the mountains and rocks gathered from the hills. But that wasn't all. Indians were camped between the settlement and the fort. There were no deerskin wigwams, only five or six lean-tos made of small tree trunks, covered with deerskins.

"Well, would you look at that," Sammy said.

"The territory's getting crowded," Lighthorse said. "The settlers built close to the fort for protection from the Apaches, and thc Apaches got between them and the fort."

"Apaches?"

"Warm Springs Apaches. This was their country, and they tried to fight off the white soldiers. But they had to fight the Chiricahuas, too, and they finally decided the soldiers were less of a threat."

"There ain't very many of 'em."

"They always were a small bunch. That made 'em easy for the Chiricahuas to kill. But there are more of 'em than this. They've had to move so much I don't know where the rest of 'em are now."

"They must be friendly or the army wouldn't allow 'em to camp here."

The partners rode through the one-street settlement, past a half-canvas, half-log structure with a crude sign hanging over a plank door. The sign read, "SALOON." Another building with a tar paper roof sported a sign that read, "GEN. MERCHANDISES." The few men they saw looked like miners and timberjacks. They nodded in a friendly fashion.

"Do you reckon they're trying to compete with the sutler?" Sammy asked.

Pointing a thumb at the saloon, Lighthorse allowed, "That gent probably gets most of his customers from the fort."

The partners were known at Fort Bayard, so they had no trouble getting inside the gate. Their first stop was at the stables, where they put up their horses; the next was at the sutler's, where they paid for their horses' keep and bought fresh steaks, bread and potatoes. Then they went to the Indian section of the fort, where they were invited to roast their steaks and potatoes over a bed of hot coals.

Though the Indians were Apache, Lighthorse managed to communicate with them through a combination of short phrases and a lot of sign language. He explained to Sammy, "Some of 'em started out following a new leader named Geronimo, but decided they didn't want to be running from the soldiers all the time."

"So if they couldn't whip 'em, they joined 'em, huh?"

"They aren't all scouts. They work for the army, cutting logs and firewood, hunting meat, hauling water and stuff like that. The women are making shirts and things out of deerskin that the sutler can send back east for a profit."

Stomachs filled, the two men went back to the stables and were pleased to see their bay horses happily munching grass hay. They spread their blankets under a long roof on poles. "They could call this the Apache Hotel," Sammy quipped.

Most of the white soldiers stayed out of the Indian section, but a few wandered over out of curiosity. One, with sergeant's stripes on his sleeves, walked straight up to the two partners.

He bellowed, "I sure didn't expect to see you two again. Lighthorse, you old blanket ass, what're you doin' these days."

"Make 'em Injun bed," Lighthorse said, grinning. "Paleface bed too soft."

"Collins, you ain't thinkin' about re-uppin', are you?"

"I thought about it—for maybe two seconds."

Squatting on his heels, the sergeant shook his head, grinning. "I don't need to ask. You didn't find Crazy Schlotman's gold mine."

"Trouble is," Sammy said, "we wouldn't know gold if it jumped up and hollered at us."

"Yeah. We probably rode over it five or six times."

"Aw, get on with you. Nobody's gonna find that mine."

"What has the army been doing? Chasing Victorio?"

"Some. We chased a bunch of 'em south into Mexico a while back. We been hearin' about a new 'Pache leader named Geronimo. He's gonna give us fits."

The two partners knew firsthand about that bunch of Apaches; but they didn't feel like telling a long story, so they didn't mention it.

"We got after 'em just in time to keep 'em from attackin' a little chickenshit town named Buckhorn. They was primed for war."

"Chickenshit is right," Lighthorse said. The sergeant didn't ask what he knew about the town, and he didn't elaborate.

"Them was a mean-lookin' bunch of jaspers. Looked like they'd cut your throat for a quarter dollar. Prob'ly should've let the 'Paches have at 'em."

"Well," Sammy said, changing the subject, "maybe some other regiment will go chasing this Geronimo."

"I hope so. I'm gettin' too old to fight Indians."

"And too fat," Lighthorse said. "You're getting an ass on you like a steamer trunk."

"Say," the sergeant said, "I just remembered. A deputy sheriff from Socorro was here askin' about you two. Said you busted out of jail up there. What all you ranihans been doin', anyhow?"

"Did he spread the word all over the fort?"

"I don't know. Asked me and a few others."

"Goddam."

"Did you bust out of jail?"

"Yeah, but we were locked up for only defending ourselves. And we didn't hurt anybody breakin' out."

"Did you get that good-lookin' woman up to Albuquerque?"

"Yeah, we did," Sammy answered, "but we got into a firefight with the same bunch that killed her husband."

"Is that what it was all about?"

"That's it."

"Well, I ain't gonna report you, and I don't think anybody else on this post is. We don't owe that deputy anything."

"I appreciate that," Sammy said. "Just the same, we'd better not hang around here too long."

"And," the sergeant said, "that 'minds me of somethin' else. That purty woman was here, too, askin' for you."

"Who?"

"That woman you left with. Mrs. Wilcox."

"What?" Sammy couldn't believe it. "Aw come on, you're jobbing."

"No. Honest. She was here, said she owed you some money."

"She sure as hell does," Lighthorse said, "but we didn't expect to ever see her again."

"Yup. She came ridin' up with an old trapper named Beaver Tunis. Said if we see you to tell you she's gonna stay in Silver City awhile."

Sammy looked at Lighthorse. Lighthorse looked at Sammy. "That do beat all," Sammy said.

After they'd eaten the rest of their steak and potatoes and shared some coffee with the Apaches, the partners relaxed on their blankets under the long roof. They had been quiet on the subject of Mrs. Wilcox, each with his own thoughts. Finally, Lighthorse asked, "Well, whatta you think?"

"I think I'll go over to Silver City and hunt her up," Sammy said. "Wanta go along?"

"Naw. I ain't forgot the last time I rode into a white man's town. I'm pretty comfortable here, long as that deputy doesn't come nosing around again."

"Well, if I collect any money from her, I'll come back and give you your share."

"I could use some cash money, all right. I'm busted."

"Here." Sammy took his thin roll of bills out of a shirt pocket and peeled off two twenties. "This won't repay you for the grub you bought, that I helped you eat, but it's half of what I've got."

"This will keep me in beans and bread for a long time." Then after a moment of silence, Lighthorse said, "You didn't happen to notice that pretty little Apache gal, did you?"

"That one in the purple dress and high-top moccasins?"

"Yeah, the one with her hair parted in the middle and combed down to her shoulders."

"Sure, I noticed her. She reminded me of how long it's been since I've had a woman."

"Aw, is that what she made you think of? Me, I thought of a warm tepee and woman cooking and, you know, stuff like that."

"Oh, yeah, I see what you mean. Well, she sure is pretty." To himself, Sammy thought, She's a little plump, but pleasantly so. Nice smile and beautiful brown eyes. To his partner he said, "How old do you reckon she is?"

"Around twenty. Old enough that she's eager to grab herself a man."

"You wouldn't be thinking—?"

Lighthorse cut him off, "No. Not me. I've got nothing to offer." He smiled wryly. "Hell, I'm wanted by the law."

Twenty

It was a seven-hour ride to Silver City. At first, Sammy couldn't shake off that scary feeling of being alone in hostile Indian country. Then he reminded himself he was in safe territory. The renegade Apaches had been chased into Mexico, and with only forty dollars in his pocket and wearing ragged clothes, he was too poor to draw the attention of road agents. Besides, he was headed for a town with hotels and restaurants, which meant a soft bed and good rations. Not rations, dammit, grub. Six miles from town he caught up with a string of eight freight wagons, each pulled by four mules, hauling supplies all the way from El Paso. He trotted on ahead of them. The town was busy, the main street loaded with more freight wagons hauling ore from the mining camps in the Mogollons, ranchers in buggies and cowboys on horseback. Riding down the main street, Sammy counted two hotels, three restaurants, three general stores, a meat market, two haberdasheries, a drug store, and a new brick bank building. Also, there were four saloons on that street.

He dismounted in front of the Exchange Hotel. As soon as he stepped inside he knew he couldn't afford to stay here. The lobby was big enough for a squad of troopers to camp in, and the walls were covered with rose-colored wallpaper. Fine, big, hand-carved Spanish-styled chairs lined the middle of the room in front of a big glass window, and a hand-carved desk with pigeonholes behind it squatted near the far wall.

Sammy walked across a wool carpet to the desk, where a wrinkled, bald little man in a stiff white collar squinted at him over the top of half-lens glasses. After taking in Sammy's short beard and badly worn clothes, he informed him coldly that rooms were rented for five dollars per night, which must be paid in advance.

Sammy had an urge to turn on his heels and leave. But on second thought, he could afford one night in a luxury hotel. He paid his five dollars and was assigned a room on the second floor overlooking an alley.

"Shit," he said to himself, looking around the sparsely furnished room, "I did better than this in Albuquerque for a dollar." He was even more disappointed when the stiff-faced clerk told him there was no bathing facility, but he could rent a tub of warm water in one of the barber shops.

"Up his ass," he muttered to himself as he went outside, mounted his horse and went looking for a livery.

But he felt better after buying a pair of stiff, new denim pants, a blue cotton shirt, one size too big to allow for shrinkage, drawers and socks, and after he'd had a shave, haircut and bath in one of the barbershops. The world looked better yet when he was served a medium-rare beefsteak with mashed potatoes, milk gravy and beans in a restaurant next door to the hotel. The only bad moment came when he passed a town marshal on the plank walk. With his heart beating too fast, he forced himself to walk casually, like a man with nothing to fear. But in his mind he wondered if the sheriff in Socorro had sent wanted flyers with descriptions of him and Lighthorse to other towns. He avoided the lawman's eyes, but he could feel the man looking at him. Not until the marshal had strolled on by did he breathe easy again. He hadn't been recognized. A cool mug of beer in the Silver Lode saloon tasted so good that he ordered another.

"Care for a game o' cards, mister?" The speaker was dressed like a miner in baggy denim pants, red suspenders and a faded, collarless shirt. But his face had seen too little weather, and his fingers wrapped around a shot glass were long with clean nails and no calluses.

"No thanks," Sammy said. He'd liked playing low stakes poker in the barracks, but he'd learned the hard way to stay out of games with professionals, especially professionals who tried to look like working stiffs.

He wondered where the whorehouses were in Silver City. Now that was something he would care for. But after mentally counting his money, he decided he couldn't afford it. Thinking about what little money he had, Sammy sipped his second beer, trying to make it last.

The smell of barbershop toilet water still clung to him as he walked on the plank walk up one side of the main street and down the other, enjoying the cool evening breeze and civilization. This was the way to live. The mountains, campfires, starry nights were fine—for a while. But he'd had his share, served his time. He'd noticed that few men in Silver City carried guns. He'd left his Remmington six-shooter in the hotel room, and he felt a little lopsided without it; but it was good to know he didn't need it. In front of a saddle shop, he stopped to admire a new saddle in the window, one with roses hand-carved in the leather skirts and fenders. He had an urge to go inside and smell the new leather, run his hands over it. But he couldn't afford to buy anything in there, so he stayed out.

The evening was still young, and maybe, he decided, he could find her.

"Nope, she ain't staying here," said the stiff-faced clerk in the Exchange Hotel lobby. Sammy thought he ought to at least check his book. The Exchange was a big hotel, the biggest Sammy had ever been in, yet this little weasel could remember who all was staying here and who wasn't. Or thought he could.

"Thanks a heap." Outside, he turned his steps toward the second biggest hotel in town, the Tremont. It was another hotel with a big lobby and well-dressed men sitting in the lobby chairs, smoking big cigars. The skinny clerk with a bow tie was another holier-than-thou who viewed the working class as something below him.

"Whom shall I say is calling?"

"She's here, then?"

"Yes."

"What room?"

The clerk's nose went up another notch. "We do not allow our guests to entertain visitors of the opposite sex."

Sammy would have been willing to bet that a couple of dollars would get her room number from this stuffed shirt. But he asked, "Can I send a message to her?"

"If you will give me your name, I will deliver a message."

He gave his name, then found a heavy, uncomfortable, straight-backed chair in the lobby as far from the other men as he could get. After a few minutes the clerk came back down the stairs and resumed studying his ledgers. Sammy walked over.

"Did you deliver my name?"

Without looking up, the clerk answered, "Of course."

"Well, what did she say?"

"I did not wait for an answer."

"Well for . . . thanks a heap." He went back to his chair and waited. Squirmed and waited. A saddle on a trotting horse was more comfortable. The Mexicans sure liked big, heavy chairs, and damn, they were hard on the ass and back.

Then, after he'd squirmed for the fifteenth time, a woman came down the stairs. A young woman in a long blue dress with big pearl buttons and lots of lace. Slender, small waist. Dark, carefully brushed, shoulder-length hair. She smiled a pretty smile when she saw him.

"Why, Mr. Collins, how wonderful to see you again."

At first he couldn't believe it. This couldn't be the woman in baggy clothes, tangled hair and haggard face he'd traveled horseback with and camped with for five or six days and nights. But when she spoke his name he could see the resemblance.

He stood, hat in hand, not able to speak for the moment.

She sat, straight, ankles crossed, feet tucked under the chair. "Please," she said, motioning to the chair next to hers. He sat, stiffly, even more uncomfortable.

"How have you been, Sammy? How is Lighthorse?"

"Why, he's, uh, we're fine." Then he remembered that this was the woman who'd lied to them, cheated them, got them into serious trouble. "What are you doing here?"

The smile left her face. "I'm here hoping you would come along. Is Lighthorse with you?"

"No, he's at Bayard."

"I wish he were here. I have something to say to the both of you."

"Yeah," Sammy said dryly. "I reckon you have. You've got some explaining to do."

"Would you care for a cup of coffee? They serve excellent coffee in the dining room."

"I can listen just as well right here."

"All right." She shifted in her chair, trying to find a comfortable position. "If you both are angry with me, I can't blame you. I do owe you some money, and I'll pay you what I can. However, my funds are limited, and I'm afraid I can't pay the promised amount."

She paused to see his reaction. His face showed nothing, but his mind was working. Sure, sure. Should have known.

"You, uh, you are no doubt wondering why I left Albuquerque without paying you. Let me explain."

Uh-huh, he thought. Go ahead. Explain. But he kept his mouth shut.

"They found me. I sold the gold to a broker, but they found me and were watching me. I did something very foolish; I took the next stage out of the city. I was terrified. You and Lighthorse were out of town, and I was alone. I tried to leave without being seen, but of course that was impossible. They caught us, four of them, and stopped the stage at gunpoint. They knew exactly what they were looking for, and they found it in a satchel I had purchased. Fortunately, I had some of the money hidden in my clothing, so they didn't get everything."

Yep, Sammy thought. This is just the kind of story I'd make up. Aloud, he asked, "So what are you doing here?"

"I came down here hoping to find you and Lighthorse. I met an elderly trapper named Beaver Tunis and paid him to accompany me. We traveled on horseback. He knows the territory very well, and he was a perfect gentleman."

"Uh-huh. Why did you want to find us?"

"I want to get my money back, and I know how to do it."

"Oh? How?"

"They robbed me and I intend to rob them."

"And you want us to help?"

"Exactly."

Shaking his head, Sammy said quickly, "Oh, no. We're already in a lot of trouble because we helped you. We won't make that mistake again."

She was silent for a long moment, studying the carpet, sitting perfectly still. Sammy cleared his throat to say something, then decided he didn't know what to say. Finally, she spoke:

"You know, you're right about being in trouble. We came through Socorro, and the sheriff there recognized me. If I'd been a man, he would have arrested me on the spot. He thinks you stole the gold we were carrying, and he said the men you killed were guards that Mr. Harrels sent to arrest you and recover it."

"Yep. That's what he thinks."

"Of course you know all this. You know you're wanted for murder and jailbreak."

"Mr. Harrels?"

"The owner of the Packrat Mine and Milling Works, and the biggest thief in the nation. He's a cold-blooded murderer himself, and he'll do anything to cheat poor prospectors out of their mining claims."

"And, of course, that's what he did to you and your husband, your late husband. He was your husband, wasn't he?"

Now her expression changed from placating to indignation to anger. Her face was red, and although she answered with only one word, she was emphatic: "Yes."

"Uhmm." His first thought was to apologize, but then he remembered what a liar she was. Finally, he said, "Well, if you'll just give me the money you owe us, I'll be on my way."

"As I said, I can't pay as much as I promised." She stood suddenly. "I'll go to my room and get my pocketbook." She left, walking with quick steps, back straight, dignified. A shapely woman.

He stood, too, stretched and stepped to the window and looked out. Dusk had settled in. Traffic on the street was lighter. An old man used a hook on a long pole to take a lantern down from a high pole. While Sammy watched, the man lighted it and hung it up again. They've got everything in this town, Sammy mused. Street lights, stores of all kinds, even a bank.

Which was more proof that she was a liar. Go to Albuquerque where there was a bank, she'd said. Hell, she didn't have to go any farther than Silver City. What she'd wanted to do was to get out of the territory.

When she came back, the anger had left her face. She was composed, and she talked with sincerity.

"Please sit down, Sammy. Perhaps I didn't explain as well as I should have." She sat. He'd rather have collected the money and left, but he sat, reluctantly, and waited to hear whatever kind of tale she would tell next.

Twenty-one

Mrs. Wilcox handed Sammy a roll of greenbacks and said, "This is a hundred dollars. If I give you any more, I'll have to go hungry."

He took the money, counted it and put it in a shirt pocket, then buttoned the pocket. "This will keep us from going hungry for a while," he said.

Hands folded in her lap, she looked into his face. Her eyes were gray, beautiful. "Let me explain. Henry, my late husband, found some color in a creek near Buckhorn. He traced it to a vein near an outcropping of quartz. He came all the way to Silver City to file a claim with the county clerk. Then we went to work, digging, chipping and doing what assaying we could with primitive methods. We realized we had something valuable. Unfortunately, Mr. Harrels realized it, too."

Sammy listened. Something in her eyes, in her face, made him a shade less doubtful.

"One day he showed up with two men. Ugly men with guns. He said he had just staked a claim there and we were trespassing. Of course, Henry told him he was mistaken and he could prove it. Harrels laughed. Just laughed. Henry came back here to the county clerk's office, and . . ." Her face started to crumple, but then she composed herself and went on:

"It seems that stealing mining claims is easy. We didn't know whether he'd bribed somebody or simply burglarized the county clerk's office. But Henry's claim could not be found. Instead there was a new claim filed by Mr. Harrels."

She was quiet while Sammy digested that. She could be telling the truth, he thought. Or she could be making up a tall tale. When it came to lying, she was an expert. Yet . . .

"All right, then, how did you get the gold you had? Stole it of course, but how?"

Smiling for a change, she said, "It was easy. You won't believe how easy it was. When Henry went to Mr. Harrels' office to plead with him, he made a mental note of the safe in the office. Henry had used some blasting powder at our mine, and we planned to blow open the safe."

Pausing a moment, she smiled again. "Our next problem was how to get the guards—two of them—away from the office, away from the mill. That was easy, too. Henry paid a young woman, an attractive young woman, a prostitute, to entice them away." Now Mrs. Wilcox chuckled. "She did her job well."

"Well, I'll be d-durned. If they'd been soldiers, they'd have been court-martialed for leaving their posts."

"Soldiers they were not. Just undisciplined thugs. The kind of men Mr. Harrels surrounds himself with. And we didn't have to blow open the safe because there were two boxes of very high grade ore right there on the office floor. All we had to do was carry them to where we had left our horses."

Sammy found himself smiling in spite of his mistrust. Either this was the truth or one of the damndest stories he'd ever heard. He waited for her to continue.

"We couldn't believe our good fortune. We were stealing, but only what was rightfully ours. The boxes fit perfectly on our pack saddle. They had leather loops and all, as if they were made for a pack saddle; probably they were. We were on our way. Only . . ." Her smile vanished. "We were not as experienced in the ways of the out-of-doors as we should have been. They caught us, and . . . you know the rest."

"Uh," Sammy grunted. "You can't hide the tracks of three horses."

She spread her hands, palms up, then let them fall into her lap. "So now you know the truth." When he didn't comment, she added, "And now you know why I want to do it again."

Sammy mulled it over, then shook his head. "Like I said, we're in trouble already. And it's because we tried to help you. Did help you. I'm afraid, Mrs. Wilcox, we're not the criminal kind."

"Will you think about it? Consider, for instance, that you are already wanted by the law for murder. Another crime, a robbery, won't make any difference."

"Naw. I'm no robber, and neither is Lighthorse."

"Don't reject me immediately. Talk it over with Lighthorse."

"I, uh, yeah, all right, I'll talk it over with Lighthorse."

"I'll stay here awhile longer. I might end up cleaning rooms for a living in the hotel where I am now a paying guest."

Sammy didn't say it, but he couldn't help thinking it:

So you might have to work for a living, so what? Yet he suspected she had been brought up in a high-class family, and though she'd worked at hard labor in their mine, doing common labor for others would be bitter medicine for her.

He asked, "What about your family? Won't they send you some money to get back to St. Louis?"

She made a wry face. "I don't know. My father . . . he didn't want me to come west with Henry. I . . . I'm not sure he would help."

"Oh." Well, he thought, it was none of his business. He said, "I'll go back to Bayard and talk it over with Lighthorse. If I'm not back within a week, forget about us."

"You . . . you aren't leaving tonight, are you?"

"No. I paid for a night in a soft bed, and I'm gonna sleep in it."

"Would you do a small favor for me? Have dinner with me? I won't talk about my problem or my plan during dinner. I promise. It's just that I would rather not have to dine alone."

"Oh, sure." He grinned. "I'll be happy to take sup— dine with you."

"Wonderful. Meet me right here in an hour, will you?"

She kept her word. Instead of talking about a robbery, she insisted on talking about him. Listening, rather. At times, during a good meal of roast beef, baked potatoes, green beans and peach cobbler, he was embarrassed. He wasn't used to answering questions about himself. But in a short time she managed to learn all about him, his background, everything but his ambition. He had to stammer over that question:

"I really don't know. I wish I did. I'd like to see more of the world than the Territory of New Mexico, and from what I've heard I have no wish to see Texas. California sounds like an interesting place. I might like to go there."

"Do you know that you can travel by rail from Denver to Cheyenne in Wyoming, and from there all the way to California?"

"No, I didn't know that."

"Yes. They just completed the transcontinental railroad."

"Well, boy, wouldn't it be grand to do that."

"As a matter of fact, I think you can travel by rail from Trinidad in the Territory of Colorado, or from Pueblo."

Shaking his head, smiling, he said, "Will wonders never cease."

The bed in the Exchange Hotel was soft—too soft. Sammy fell onto its thick feather mattress and immediately felt like he was being smothered. He tried all positions. Lying on his stomach put a curve in his back, lying on his back put his feet higher than his head, and lying on his side put a crook in his neck. A blanket on the ground was more comfortable.

"Aw hell," he muttered to himself, "you just ain't used to living like a white man. You paid for it, dammit, so get used to it."

He'd been looking forward to the pleasure of sleeping late, but by daylight he was up and getting dressed. Breakfast was good, though. Eggs over easy, ham, biscuits and butter, fried potatoes, coffee. He sat at a long counter in a workingman's cafe and lingered over break-fast and coffee. He paid and strolled leisurely to the livery pens to collect his horse, knowing he had plenty of time to ride back to Fort Bayard.

But before he got to the livery pens he changed his mind.

Was that town of Buckhorn as mean as he thought, or did the citizens there just hate Indians? Did that gent named Harrels really steal mining claims from prospectors? If he went there, had a drink in the saloon, would he be recognized?

Curiosity killed the cat, he reminded himself. It could kill me, too, but, aw hell, was that woman telling the truth?

He turned his steps to the General Merchandise, where he bought a stack of corn tortillas, two cans of beans and a two-inch-thick slice of cured ham. At the livery pens, he stuffed his groceries in his saddlebags, saddled his horse and rode out of town. But instead of going northeast to Fort Bayard, he went northwest toward Buckhorn.

The rocky wagon road he followed wound through scrub oak, piñon, juniper and mahogany trees. He believed he could travel at a walk, save his horse's strength, and still get there before dark. Climbing steadily, he soon found himself among thousands of yellow pines and stands of alders and mountain maples. Stopping beside a creek that ran out of a thicket of wild cherries, he loosened his saddle cinch, hobbled his horse and ate two of the tortillas. Horseback again, he rode on, meeting no one. At sundown he came to the big ponderosa on the edge of Buckhorn, the tree he believed was the hanging tree. Instead of riding down the one street, he rode around the town, climbing a low hill, and stopped about two hundred yards from the big, rambling building that was the Packrat Mine & Milling Works.

Heavy black smoke billowed out of a high rock chimney and floated over the town. From where he sat his horse, Sammy could see a door with a sign over it that read: "OFFICE."

So this was the place. Looking around him, he saw a brushy ravine going downhill from the building toward town. To the west were the higher mountains, to the north a pine-covered trough between hills. That had to be where Henry Wilcox and his wife had left their horses. Sammy rode over to it. It was a good spot, hidden from the office door.

Dark was coming on fast. He rode north around behind the mill to the creek that came tumbling down out of the high hills. It was the creek that supplied water for the milling works. And it was a good place to spend the night. He off-saddled the bay gelding, hobbled it and let it graze on a grassy bank of the creek while he ate two more tortillas and a piece of the ham. Before he rolled up in his blankets he had to have a look at that office.

Moving as quietly as he could in the light of a quarter moon, he worked his way down to the west end of the mill to where he believed he could see the office door— if he could see anything. The building was nothing more than a big dark shape in the dim moonlight. Sammy stood still, straining his eyes and listening. The mill had been shut down for the night, and not a sound came from it. If the office was lighted, the window was covered. If it had a window.

Listened. He sucked in his breath sharply when a match flared not more than seventy feet in front of him. The match lit a cigarette—and illuminated a man's face. A bearded face under a floppy, dark hat. The match went out, but the cigarette glowed brighter as the man sucked on it. The glow made a slow arc down, then back up where it brightened, then down again.

The woman was right, this guard was no soldier. His cigarette gave away his location. An Indian could walk up to him in the dark and cut his throat.

Was there only one man on guard? Naw, there had to be more than one. The woman said there were two. The other had to be in the office where the safe was supposed to be. Sure enough, a door opened, allowing dim lamplight to spill out. A man stood in the door, making a perfect target of himself. He said something. The gent with the cigarette said something. The door closed.

Silently, Sammy worked his way back to his camp. In the moonlight, he could see the shape of his horse grazing along the creek. By feel, he unrolled his blankets, pulled off his boots and lay on his back with one blanket under him and another covering him up to his chin. What had he learned? Nothing much. Everything he'd seen was just the way the woman had described it.

So what was he doing here? Lying on his back, gazing at the stars between the treetops, he had no ready answer for his own question. Curiosity? Yeah, sure, just curious was all. Why curious? He couldn't be interested in Mrs. Wilcox's plan. Naw. Not really. Still, it was kind of intriguing, if nothing else.

Yeah, that was the word: *intriguing*.

Twenty-two

After breakfast, Sammy decided to do some exploring before he went back to Fort Bayard. He couldn't make it to the fort in one day from here anyway, not without riding hard, so he figured he had some time to kill. He rode up the creek a few miles until he came to where another, smaller, stream joined that one. He followed the smaller stream a few miles, then saw a tent.

It was a good-sized tent, about fifteen by fifteen, with a stovepipe sticking out one end. The two men saw him before he saw them, and they had rifles in their hands. Sammy reined up. The two were working a sluice box in front of their tent, but they'd kept rifles handy. Handy and ready. Both had full beards. One wore a ragged, narrow-brim hat and the other a bill cap.

Sammy hollered, "Morning."

They didn't answer. The rifles weren't pointed at him, but the men were holding them in such a way that they could snap them up to their shoulders in a second. Sammy held his right hand up, hopefully to show he meant no harm, and rode forward. When he was closer, he again said, "Morning."

One of the men nodded, spat a stream of tobacco juice, and answered, "Mornin'."

Sammy rode on until he was about twenty feet from them. "I'm harmless," he said. "I'm just looking the country over."

Their eyes took in the six-shooter in its flap holster, and the one in the bill cap asked, "You by yourself?"

"Yep."

"Whar you comin' from?"

"Fort Bayard. I was in the Sixth Cavalry, but I took my honorable a while back."

The two shuffled their feet and relaxed a little, but held on to their rifles. "Well, light, if you want to."

Dismounted, Sammy said, "I'm curious about prospecting. I know nothing about it. Is that a sluice box?"

"Yep." Another squirt of tobacco juice splattered on the ground.

"I've heard of 'em, and I think I know how they work. I was wondering, though, how do you file a claim if you find something?"

"Down to the county seat."

"Silver City?"

"Yup."

"I suppose you have to have a good description and sign some papers."

"Yup."

"With the county clerk, I suppose. I've heard of the clerk losing the papers."

The gent in the ragged hat asked, "You say you're from Bayard?"

"I was there, yeah, then my company went up to Fort Union. I've got a partner camped at Bayard who wants to do some prospecting. I hope you don't mind my questions."

Putting his rifle butt on the ground, the gent continued

squinting at Sammy and said, "I'd invite you to a cup of java, but the pot's empty and the fire's out."

"I don't need any coffee anyhow. Fact is, I'd better get going back to Bayard. I was wondering, though, I've been told that papers have been missing from the county clerk's office and somebody has been stealing claims."

"Yup."

"Is there any way to protect your claim?"

"Wal, what we done is we got a feller in Silver City to stake us to some grub and stuff, and him and the town marshal witnessed it when we filed."

"Oh, yeah, that would work."

"You ain't a detective, are you?"

Grinning, Sammy said, "No. I'm just curious. Judging from what I've been told, though, I wish I was a lawman. I'd try to get the goods on this Mr. Harrels. He's the one doing the claim stealing, isn't he?"

"He's the one."

"Well"—Sammy mounted the bay—"you men did the smart thing, getting witnessees. If my pardner and I ever file a claim, that's what we'll do." Before he turned the horse around, he said, "I hope you both get rich."

Instead of riding around the town, Sammy reined up and looked down at it. The wagon track from the Pack-rat mill was well-traveled, but rocky. The town was quiet with no traffic on the street and only a few men walking from one place to another. Two men went into the saloon. Early drinkers, Sammy thought. He guessed that the building with log walls and a roof made of one-inch lumber covered with tar paper was a cafe. Two men came out, picking their teeth, and another went in.

What would he gain by going down there? Nothing. Except maybe to get another look at the kind of people who lived there. What difference would that make? Not much. But . . .

Without trying to answer his own question, Sammy turned his horse downhill and rode onto the wagon tracks coming from the mill. He rode at a walk onto the one street, between badly constructed buildings, and stopped before the saloon. Some of the houses, he noticed, were built off the ground, on thick logs or rock foundations. Must have been some flooding from the creek at some time or other, he mused. Two saddled horses stood tied at a hitch rail in front of the saloon.

Sammy got down and wrapped the reins once around the hitch rail, then stepped inside the saloon. Only three customers stood at the bar. Except for what they wore on their heads, they all looked alike: full beards, baggy britches held up with suspenders, six-guns in holsters on their hips or inside their waist bands. Two had shapeless, wide-brim hats on their heads, and the other wore a pillbox cap. They looked him over with unfriendly eyes, and didn't care whether he liked it or not.

"Beer," he said to the barman, whose beard was as wild as everyone else's.

The barman stared at him a moment, then turned and drew a mug of beer from a keg mounted behind the bar. "Six bits."

"How much?"

With his hands on the bar, his face close to Sammy's, the barman growled, "I said six bits. You deef?"

Sammy nodded at other mugs of beer on the bar. "Is that what they paid?"

"Are you gonna pay or ain't you?"

"No," Sammy said, shaking his head. "I never paid that much for a beer in my life and I ain't going to now."

The mug was snatched off the bar. "Then get yur ass outta here."

"He's a troublemaker," said one of the customers.

"Shore is. He's one a them nicety-nice fellers from somewhar east."

"I seen 'im afore. Ain't he the one that helped that redskin get away."

"Yep, by God, I b'lieve he is."

"Good day to you all," Sammy said, turning to the door.

Outside, he cursed himself for being so stupid as to come here. He was reaching for the reins of his horse when a harsh voice came from behind him. "Hold up, thar. You ain't goin' nowhar."

Sammy turned and faced them. The three of them. No, the four of them. The barman was coming outside, too. One of the customers, with a six-gun holstered low on his right hip, stepped up.

"Best you jest hand over that thar pistola that you carry in that thar army kind of leather."

None of the four had guns in their hands, but they knew they could draw their guns faster than he could get his pistol out of the flap holster. It occurred to him that maybe they wanted him to reach for his gun, give them an excuse to kill him.

A cold knot of fear formed in Sammy's stomach. Four of them. He believed he could shoot as well as any of them, but he'd never practiced the fast draw. He felt his knees going weak with fear.

"Haw, haw. He's about to pee his britches."

The nearest one stepped even closer, put his ugly face close to Sammy's. "Hand 'er over."

"N-no, I . . . ." He'd had no experience in street shooting, but street brawling was old stuff. That was something he'd had to learn on the streets of Chicago. He gulped and tried to force down the fear. Maybe they did all their fighting with guns here. Maybe a punch in the eye would surprise the hell out of them.

The ugly one's hand went to his own gun, started to draw it out. Something in Sammy's mind screamed: "DO IT NOW."

With his left hand he grabbed the man's gun, and with his right, he hit him in the left eye. The man staggered back a step, but Sammy stayed with him, and hit him again. And again with a right cross, then whipped his right elbow back and hit the ugly one in the right eye, hard.

Now he had the man's six-gun in his left hand with the hammer back. He poked the bore into the man's stomach. "Halt," he yelled at the other three. "Halt or I'll shoot him."

They had their guns out, but Sammy kept the ugly one between him and them. He yelled again, "One move and he's dead." They stopped, eyes wide.

"Put down those guns. Do it, or by God I'll put a bullet in his guts and get at least one of you."

They hesitated, looked at one another. Talking through his teeth, Sammy hissed, "You've got about five seconds. Then he's dead."

The bartender was the first. Squatting, he carefully placed his six-gun on the dirt path in front of the saloon. One by one, the other two did the same, all staring bullets at Sammy.

"Now get back. Get away from 'em."

They stepped back.

"Farther. Do it. I can shoot you all down now."

They stepped back farther.

Sammy shoved the ugly one, the one with the bloody face, toward them. Then watching them carefully, he picked up their six-guns. His biggest fear was the possibility of someone coming up behind him. He wanted to get on his horse and ride like hell, but he had his hands full of guns. He couldn't just stand there. Sooner or later someone would come along. A quick look around, and his eyes took in a gap in the rock foundation under the saloon.

"Don't move," he warned. "One little move and I start blasting." He knelt before the gap and threw the pistols through it and under the saloon, one at a time. Standing, shifting Bloody Face's gun to his right hand, he reached for his pocket knife with his left and opened the blade with his teeth. Then he cut the reins of the two horses standing beside his bay gelding at the hitch rail. The two horses turned away, walked away, then broke into a trot. The bay gelding wanted to follow, but Sammy grabbed the reins.

Still watching the four uglies, he stepped into the saddle, turned his horse east and booted him into a gallop. A hundred yards up the street he dropped the ugly one's gun and hazarded a look back. One of the four was crawling through the gap in the foundation. They'd be armed again.

"All right, feller," Sammy said to the bay, "let's move on the double." With his spurless boot heels, he urged the horse into a dead run, and soon left the town of Buckhorn behind.

Twenty-three

It took the rest of that day and most of the next to reach Fort Bayard. Sammy quit the wagon tracks a few miles out of Buckhorn and traveled across country, through the few ponderosas and thousands of yellow pines, down to the scrub oak and cedars. He repeatedly studied his back trail and also the country ahead of him. There could still be some Apaches around, and those uglies in Buckhorn could be so mad they'd trail him to hell and back. Chuckling to himself, he wondered what kind of tale they'd tell, what excuse they'd make for letting one man disarm them and escape. He camped away from any stream, back in the pines where he couldn't be found in the dark, then was riding again shortly after first light.

She was on his mind, too. A beautiful woman. A woman with class. Every man's dream. She'd been as sweet as pie and had kissed him on the cheek when he'd left her at her hotel room door. Did that mean anything? Naw, not what he hoped it meant. What it meant, he told himself, was she needed his help. Nothing more. That's what he told himself.

But wouldn't it be grand, wouldn't it be heaven just to . . . ?

Naw. Forget it, Sammy Collins.

* * *

Lighthorse Jones had built a lean-to shelter just outside the fort, near the camp of the Warm Springs Apaches. They knew he was a Ute; but the little tribe had never quarreled with the Utes, and they treated him with respect. He made it a point to accidentally-on-purpose meet with the pretty Apache girl, and managed to get into pigeon-talk, hand-signaling conversations with her. The more they talked, the better they understood each other. Even her father, a skinny, bow-legged old man who wore his long hair in a knot behind his head, gave him a snaggle-toothed grin.

The girl's name in English was Little Wren. Lighthorse tried to explain why he had two names. The army, he said, insisted on keeping records of everyone who worked for it, and he had to have a first name and a last name. An officer named him Jones just to have something to put in the records. The officer got his name backward. It should have been Jones Lighthorse, instead of Lighthorse Jones, but Lighthorse didn't care and didn't try to correct it.

Getting acquainted with Little Wren made him worry even more about his future. A man needed a woman. He needed a woman to cook, keep his wigwam clean, raise his children. And he needed a woman to share his bed.

It was impossible. An Indian wanted by the law for murder had two choices. He might marry her and take her to live on the Ute reservation up north and hope he wouldn't be found there. Or he could spend years running and hiding. It wasn't enough to offer. She might agree; but her father wouldn't, and Lighthorse wouldn't blame him. Not only that, the sheriff or his deputy from Socorro could come back to the fort looking for him. Or send letters to law officers all over the west asking them to arrest him on sight. And kill him if he resisted arrest.

Impossible.

That was what Lighthorse had on his mind when Sammy found him. He smiled and was truly happy to see his partner, but Sammy sensed his depression. Sensed it but knew there was nothing he could say that would help, so he said nothing. He shared Lighthorse's camp and turned his horse out with the Indians' horses. Lighthorse allowed he'd have to go hunting and bring back some meat. This time he'd share it, and none of it would be wasted. By evening the next day they'd shot a turkey and a doe in the Pinos Altos. Lighthorse quickly gutted the doe and hung the carcass from a tree with a stick propped in the rib cage to keep it open so it would air out. Then they dressed out the turkey and put all but the two drumsticks in a burlap bag to soak in a creek. The drumsticks and a can of beans made their supper. Next morning, with the deer carcass draped behind the cantle of Sammy's saddle, they went back to the Indian camp.

There, Lighthorse held back a hindquarter and gave the rest to Little Wren and her father, who kept a fore-quarter and shared the rest with their neighbors. Meat wouldn't keep longer than two or three days down here on the lower elevations, but everything except the hooves was used for something. The sinews made bow strings, some of the bone was shaped for arrowheads, and more of the bone fed the camp's dogs. The brain was used to tan the hide. Animal skins tanned by the

Indian women were softer, prettier and more durable than anything produced by the commercial tanneries.

The two partners tried to be cheerful and pretend everything was going well, but on the third day, after eating a meal of roast venison and baked potatoes, they had to talk about the future. The hundred dollars Sammy had collected from Mrs. Wilcox wouldn't last forever; sooner or later they were going to have to do something.

"What we ought to do," Sammy said, "is go to California. I don't know if what money we've got will stretch that far or not, but I can find work somewhere between here and there."

"Yeah." Lighthorse was lying on his back with his hands under his head. "I remember the schoolteacher talking about California, and what sticks in my mind is what he said about the different races of people there."

"I remember that, too. People come from across the sea to California. A lot of different languages are spoken there. The Chinee go to California in droves. An Indian wouldn't be out of place. And the law officers wouldn't find us."

"They're gonna find us here if we stick around long enough. Any day now, one or two of 'em will ride through this camp and recognize me. If I see 'em coming, I can make myself hard to find, but they'll get an interpreter and ask questions. Then I'll be on the run again."

"We. We'll be running. They want me, too."

Lighthorse crossed his ankles, and grunted, "Unh. California would be a good place to go. I wish we was there. But it's a hell of a long ways, and like you said our money won't stretch that far. You can find work, but I can't. Not 'til we get out of this territory and across Arizona Territory and close to the Pacific Ocean. Or is it the Atlantic? No, it's the Pacific."

"If that woman had paid me what she owes us, we'd have enough money." Sammy was silent a moment, then asked, "What do you think about her scheme? You know, to rob that mill and that Mr. Harrels?"

"I'm no robber and neither are you."

"Yeah, but . . . I told you about what a robber that Harrels is himself. She told me and so did two prospectors. And that town, that Buckhorn. A stranger can't even buy a beer without those toughs jumping on him like a pack of hounds on a coyote."

"I've got a score to settle there. But, I don't reckon I ever will."

"Mrs. Wilcox said every other Thursday is payday at the mill, and most of the men in that town work at the mill. Would it bother your conscience if we stole their payroll?"

Chuckling, Lighthorse said, "I don't think so. In fact, it wouldn't bother my conscience to take everything they've got and leave 'em barefoot in the winter."

"There must be some good folks in that town, but if there are, they make themselves scarce."

"Naw. There ain't any good folks in Buckhorn. Nobody came along and tried to talk those toughs into letting me go. Nobody cared. Everyone I saw was having fun. They were licking their chops just thinking about watching me strangle to death. Naw, I've got only two words for the whole damned town, and 'Go to hell' is both of 'em."

"So, is it worth thinking about, or should we just forget it?"

"Hell, I don't know how to rob anybody."

"What Mrs. Wilcox and her husband—her late husband—planned to do was blow open the safe. They got a whore to show her ass or tits or something to get the guards away. But they found some ore that was mostly pure gold in some pack boxes outside the safe, and all they had to do was pick 'em up and carry 'em to their packhorse."

"Why were the boxes outside the safe? That kind of luck is hard to believe."

"She thinks somebody delivered 'em, but didn't have a key to open the safe, and Mr. Harrels wasn't there."

"You can bet we wouldn't have that kind of luck."

"What I'm thinking is, with all that payroll money, we can leave the gold and just take the cash. Gold is too heavy to carry on a saddle horse, and we can travel faster without a packhorse."

"Where would we go?"

"I don't know. California. Or maybe El Paso, or hell, you name it."

"Does she know how to blow open a safe? I don't."

"They had a plan, and she didn't intend to stand back and let him do it by himself; so I guess she knows how."

"Do you believe her?"

At that, Sammy had to think a moment. He answered hesitantly, "Well, yeah, I sort of believe she was telling me the truth."

"Then why did she lie to us about how she came by that gold?"

"Would we have helped her if she'd told us the gold was stolen?"

"No, but . . . yeah, I reckon she had to lie about that.

But do you believe her story about why she left Albuquerque without paying us?"

"I've been thinking about that. She could be telling the truth or she could be lying. I don't know. I do believe she was robbed of the money. Otherwise, she wouldn't have come back here."

Lighthorse sat up, crossed his legs, put his elbows on his knees and his chin in his hands. "She got lucky enough to rob the mill once; does she really believe she can do it again?"

"She thinks so. She rode a horse a long ways to do it."

"She's a pretty rugged gal."

Grinning in the dim light of a dying campfire, Sammy said, "You should have seen her there in Silver City. She looks like high society. Talks it, too. And I mean she's one damned good-looking woman."

"Personally, I like a little more meat on my women, but that's neither here nor there. What worries me is she can be two different people, and she fooled the hell out of us. She got us in serious trouble once and she could do it again."

"That's something else I've been thinking about." Sammy chuckled. "I've been thinking so much my head feels like a war drum. The way I see it, we're already in so much trouble we could be hung. Hell, they can't hang us twice."

"Unh. Well, she can't do it by herself, but I can't believe she came all the way down here to find us. She had no idea where we were."

"She says she wanted to pay us. She had hoped to find somebody else to help her, but she doesn't know how to go about finding two other men. She won't go inside a saloon and ask questions, and she doesn't know who she can trust."

"What's she gonna do if we don't do it?"

Shrugging, Sammy said, "Either she'll take a chance on two other yahoos or give up."

Lighthorse stood, walked away out of the firelight and drained his bladder, then came back and plopped down on his blankets. "You sound like you've talked yourself into it, pardner."

Sammy didn't say anything for a while. When he spoke again, he changed the subject. "Next time I see some women washing clothes, I'm gonna give 'em these new britches. Maybe they'll feel better after they've been scrubbed."

"They're washing clothes the white woman's way now with scrub boards and washtubs."

"Pardner, don't let me talk you into anything you don't feel right about."

"To tell the truth, I don't feel right about any damned thing, but this comes closer than anything else."

Twenty-four

Taking a bath in an Indian camp wasn't for the modest. Sammy borrowed a washtub and an iron kettle to heat some water in, then waited until dark to strip and get into the tub. He'd lathered, scrubbed, rinsed off and was standing in the tub, wiping himself dry with a clean flour sack, when three Indian women came by. One was Little Wren. Light from a cooking fire made him plainly visible. The women stopped, giggled, pointed at his efforts to cover himself with the sack, and, laughing now, talked among themselves in their native language.

"Goddammit," Sammy growled, "ain't you got any manners?"

That only brought more laughter. Lighthorse, squatting by the fire, laughed with them.

"Well, what's so damned funny?"

"You are. The way you're trying to cover yourself up, and your white hide."

"Hell, ain't they ever seen a white man before?"

"Not naked. Your face and hands are sun-browned, but the rest of you is snow-white."

"Well, what the hell did they expect?"

Still laughing, Lighthorse said, "They didn't know how white a white man is 'til now."

"Tell 'em to git. I ain't here to put on a show."

Lighthorse uttered a few words in their language and gesticulated with his hands, laughing at the same time. They walked away, giggling. Quickly, Sammy pulled on his freshly washed drawers, denim pants and shirt.

"Goddam," he said, "I'll never get used to bivouacing with women and kids. Hell, every time I take a crap I have to hide behind something and yell when I hear somebody coming."

"You live like this all your life and you get used to it. They don't think anything of it and neither should you."

"Yeah, well."

"If you think they got a kick out of seeing you naked, you should have heard 'em when they washed your drawers. They'd never seen anything like 'em, and they had a lot of fun making comments about 'em. They had to show 'em to everybody in the camp."

"Don't they wear underpants?"

"Naw. But the men, now, they were wondering if they could trade for some white man's drawers. They gotta keep their dinguses from swinging in the breeze, and cotton beats the hell out of leather."

"Yeah, well."

The same pompous desk clerk in the Tremont Hotel gave Sammy the same looking over, before saying coldly, "I shall go and see if the lady is in and if she wants to see you."

"Thanks a pile."

She was in and happy to see him. "Sammy," she exclaimed as she came down the stairs. "How wonderful."

She was holding her long, gray skirt off the steps with one hand and carrying a parasol with the other. Her shirtwaist was light blue with pleats, big pearl buttons and padded shoulders.

Sammy stood and admired her. When she kissed him on the cheek his whole face tingled. "We, uh, Lighthorse and me, we're camped outside town a ways. Lighthorse doesn't want to come in the town."

"Oh?" Her eyebrows went up. "Why not?"

"Some folks in this territory hate Indians, and they don't know a friendly Ute from a Chiricahua."

"Oh, I see. That's terrible."

"It is for a fact."

"Can we sit over here? I hope you've got some good news."

They occupied two chairs as far from the front desk as they could get. He sat stiffly with his hat in his hands, and she sat with her ankles crossed, feet under the chair, and her hands in her lap. "I don't know if it's good news or not. We, uh, would like to talk more about your, uh, plan."

"Of course, but where?"

"That's a problem, with you dressed the way you are."

"Yes, and if I changed to a divided skirt, old Rubber Neck over there"—she nodded in the direction of the desk clerk—"would ask why."

"Well, the only place I can think of is behind the livery barn. There's a water trough there and it's dark at night. I can come meet you here and walk over there with you."

"That will have to do."

"Yeah, I'll camp with 'im. We're used to it."

"I don't suppose you'd care to have dinner with me again?"

"No, it wouldn't be right, me eating beefsteak and Lighthorse living on Indian bread and canned beans."

"Soon, you can both be living in luxury."

"I doubt that. Not 'til we get far away from the Indian wars, and from the sheriff of Socorro County."

"Oh, yes, there is that. I'm truly sorry about that."

"Did you say every other Thursday is payday at the Packrat mill?"

"Yes. I'm sure of it. It has been for at least a year."

"How big of a payroll do they have?"

"We—Henry and I—calculated between four thousand five hundred and five thousand."

"That much? How do you figure it?"

"Last spring Mr. Harrels had one hundred and ten men—miners and mill workers—on his payrolls. Their pay seems to average twenty dollars a week. Two weeks' pay for that many men comes to four thousand four hundred dollars. Plus he has his own cash in the safe plus money for other expenses, such as machinery and the like."

"How did you get all this information?"

That brought a chuckle from her. "Henry got it. Don't ask how . . . well, all right, I'll tell you. If you want to know what's going on in a place like that, ask the local, uh, prostitutes. They know everything. Most men are chatterboxes when they're with women. Most, but not you, of course."

Sammy chuckled with her. "You let your husband go to a, uh . . ." He left his question unfinished. But she touched his arm, smiled and answered:

"It wasn't because he needed anything, you know, but

they do serve liquor in that house, at a terrific price, of course, and he went there several times to drink. And to listen."

"Uh-huh."

"Henry wasn't a stranger in Buckhorn, and no one asked embarrassing questions of him."

"Well, didn't they know he had a, uh, wife?"

"So did some of the other men. That's not unusual at all."

"No, I guess not. Anyway, you're sure that if we bust open the safe at the Packrat mill next Wednesday night, we'll find a lot of cash money in it?"

"Reasonably sure. And if by chance I'm mistaken, you will find some gold dust, which is light and just as easy to spend in these frontier towns."

"We're planning on traveling light."

"Where are you planning to go?"

Just in case she couldn't be trusted, he didn't want to tell her. But he didn't have to lie. "We haven't decided yet. What about you?"

"To St. Louis, but by a different route. I'll sell my horse and travel by stagecoach to El Paso and go from there. I could deposit my share in the bank here and write drafts on it, but I don't want to arouse any suspicion. Silver City is too close to Buckhorn, and the news will spread rapidly."

Sammy shook his head with a wry smile. "But you'll be carrying cash again."

"True, but this time I'll have my money better hidden. I can hide paper money in my clothing." Smiling, she added, "A bachelor like you has no idea how many big petticoats some women wear. We can hide anything."

"That's the way to do it, then. There has to be a bank

in El Paso, and I reckon you can cash a bank draft anywhere?"

"Anywhere there's a bank. Of course it takes time. Perhaps several weeks. You need to keep enough cash on hand to allow for that."

"One more question, then I have to go. How did you plan to blow open that safe?"

Smiling, she said, "That should be the easy part. Henry had had enough experience to know how to use blasting powder, and when he was in the mill office he noticed that the safe had a big keyhole. Not big enough to put a stick of powder in it, but big enough to put a small homemade bomb in it."

"Homemade?"

"That's easy, too. What we did was we melted a candle for the wax and rolled the wax into a small sheet. We put a small pile of black powder in the middle of the sheet, added a short fuse, then rolled the sheet up into a ball."

She paused to see if he was following her. Sammy nodded.

"Henry kept the wax ball warm and soft by holding it in his hand. We planned to fill the keyhole with it, light the fuse and get behind Mr. Harrels' desk."

"But it turned out you didn't have to do it that way."

"No. We didn't want to make any more noise than necessary, and as it was we didn't have to make any noise at all."

Sammy turned his hat brim around in his hands while he thought it over. Then he said, "Oh, yeah, I almost forgot, how are you planning to get the guards away from the office? We don't want any shooting or killing."

"Of course, I can't recruit a prostitute as Henry did,

and being a stranger in Buckhorn you can't either. But I have a plan. Believe me, I will entice them away."

"But you . . . ? How?"

"Believe me, I will."

Glancing through the lobby's big window, Sammy could see daylight fading fast. "All right. Lighthorse might have some questions. I'll meet you again right here in two hours and take you to him."

"Fine. I'll be here. And, Sammy." Her gray eyes locked onto his. "I'm so glad you came back."

Sammy went to the butcher shop and bought another thick slice of ham. Then he rode out of town. It was dark when he located Lighthorse. Rather, Lighthorse located him. Sammy rode so close to his partner that Lighthorse hit him with a small rock.

"Damn," Sammy said. "Even with a half-moon you're hard to find."

"Unh. Injun know how to hide."

"I hope so. It would be better if nobody saw us here."

"Hide 'em horses big problem."

"Yeah, that's the problem, all right. That's why I want to get this job done as soon as we can."

"What did you learn?"

"She's got it planned pretty good. I asked every question I could think of. But I told her you'd meet her behind the livery barn right soon and ask some questions of your own. I'll have to escort her there."

While they sat cross-legged on the ground and ate ham and Indian bread, Sammy told his partner everything the woman had told him. "Think it'll work?" he asked.

"I don't know." Lighthorse's face was mostly hidden in the light of a half-moon. "There's a lot of parts to it. Where there's that many parts, something is liable to not fit right."

"That's so. First, we can only hope she's right about the company payroll money being in the safe; then we can only hope she gets the guards out of the way; then we have to blow open the safe; then we have to get away."

"Yup."

"Well." Sammy stood. "Let's go talk to her and see what you think."

Behind the livery barn was a wooden trough filled with water piped from a nearby stream. They let their horses drink, and Lighthorse washed his face. He said, "I'll be somewhere around, but not right here. I'll see you or hear you when you get back."

She was waiting, wearing a divided skirt and a plain blue shirtwaist. Sammy took a seat next to hers in the hotel lobby and held his hat in his hands. "Lighthorse is behind the barn somewhere. He'll find us."

"Good. Let's stroll over that way."

Stroll, they did, as if they were out for a walk in the cool of the evening. She made small talk. "Oh, isn't it lovely out? So nice and cool. And look at the moon; it seems to be smiling down on us."

"Yeah."

Out of sight of the lamplight, their steps quickened, and soon they were behind the barn and close to the water trough. They stood there a few seconds before they heard Lighthorse's whisper. He was waiting, holding the horses, in the shadows of a few short pines.

"Good evening, Mrs. Wilcox," he said pleasantly.

"Good evening, Lighthorse. It's wonderful to see you again. Even though I can barely see you."

"Step into my parlor."

"Why, thank you. I don't mind if I do."

"I've been hearing a lot about you. Is it true, or was Sammy telling tall tales?"

"It's hard to believe, but it's true."

They stood in the dark shadows, and she told Lighthorse everything she'd told Sammy.

"Sounds like you've got it all figured put," Lighthorse said.

"I've had a lot of time to think about it."

"Well, Sammy and I, we have to do some more thinking about it, too."

"I understand. But please let me know as soon as possible. I need to know."

"Will tomorrow morning be soon enough?"

"Tomorrow morning will be fine."

With their horses hobbled, they lay on their backs on their blankets and looked at the sky. The stars were so thick that Sammy wondered why they didn't bump into one another. Lighthorse reminded him of what the schoolteacher at Fort Union had once said: They looked close from the earth, but they were thousands of miles apart.

Sammy asked, "What do you think?"

"What do you think?"

"It's your ass as much as mine."

"Uh-huh. So what do you think?"

"I think we ought to do it. What do you think?"

"Let's do it."

Twenty-five

He didn't have to send the desk clerk upstairs for her. She was sitting alone in the hotel lobby, a worried frown on her face. The frown turned to a wide smile when Sammy told her. "Wonderful." Her face turned serious. "Tomorrow is Wednesday. We have no time to waste."

"Sure. Here's our plan. Like I already told you, I went over there and scouted the place. I could see where you and your husband left your horses. It's a good spot, out of sight of everything, but close to the mill. I described it to Lighthorse, and he'll start over there alone early in the morning. We'll be right behind him. As soon as it's dark, we'll do the job. We ought to get there early enough to let our horses graze and rest so they'll be fresh and ready to travel."

"I'll be ready first thing in the morning. Will you meet me here or somewhere else?"

"Might as well meet you here. I don't know what you're gonna tell old Long Nose over there; maybe you're gonna ride to Fort Bayard with me to visit your husband's grave, or something like that. You said you still own a horse?"

"Oh, yes, I rode down here from Albuquerque on a good sound mare, and I'm keeping her at the livery."

"Good. Then I won't have to buy you a horse. What we don't have, though, is some wax and fuse."

"I have a candle in my room."

"Good. Lighthorse has got some black gunpowder and a couple of percussion caps that he talked an Indian friend out of. We don't know how much it'll take to blast open the safe. Do you?"

"Not exactly. Henry had a tin matchbox full. I suppose gunpowder is about as explosive as black blasting powder."

"It'll durn sure explode."

"And Henry had a blasting cap on the end of the fuse. He said it wouldn't take much to wreck the, uh, tumblers, he called them, in the lock."

Sammy shook his head. "It has to work. If it doesn't, we're taking a big risk for nothing."

"Henry was certain it would work."

"The only other thing we need, then, is some fuse. Not much, just a couple feet. But I don't want to go to a store and buy it. I don't want anybody curious."

"It's up to me, then. I think I know how to steal some. When I was in the mercantile across the street— just yesterday—to buy a needle and some thread, I saw a roll of fuse on the floor at the end of the counter. If I had a sharp knife, and if I could somehow distract the clerk's attention, I could cut off a piece."

"You could send him to the storage room for something. Offhand, I don't know what. That is, if there's nobody else in the store. And I'll lend you my folding knife. You can carry it in your pocketbook."

"All right. I'll get some fuse somehow."

"We have to have it."

"I'll get it. I promise."

"I'm going over to the store to buy some provisions. If there's anything you want to take along—to eat or wear or anything—you'll have to pick it out. Take some grub. Food. Put it in your saddlebags. We're not taking a packhorse."

"I can see the store from the window here, and when I see that there are no other customers, I'll go in."

Standing, Sammy said loud enough for the desk clerk to hear, "I'll meet you here in the morning. It's not a long ride to Fort Bayard." The nosy clerk heard, no doubt about that.

"I'll be ready."

Sammy crossed the street, stepped up onto a wide porch and entered the long board-and-batten building with the General Store sign over the porch roof. A bell on a spring over the door tinkled when he opened and closed the door. The clerk looked at him through thick glasses, and said, "I'll be with you in a minute, sir." While his two women customers watched, he resumed measuring a piece of cotton dress material. He used a pair of scissors to cut a yard and a half off a roll.

While he was doing that, Sammy's eyes went back and forth across the big room. Sure enough, a roll of fuse sat on the floor at the end of the counter. Out of habit, Sammy reached for his pocket knife, then remembered he'd given it to Mrs. Wilcox. Damn. He waited patiently while the clerk sold the dress material to the two women. Finally, they left.

"Yes sir?" the clerk said, stepping behind a long counter. Sammy ordered a slab of cured bacon, two stacks of tortillas, a dozen potatoes and six onions, a sack of dried apricots, another of ginger snaps and two pounds of beef jerky.

While the clerk was scurrying, collecting it all, Sammy eyed the door, hoping no one else came in. Then, "Will that be all, sir?"

"Oh," Sammy said, "I forgot to bring something to carry it in. Would you have an empty gunnysack I could borrow or buy?"

"Why, I believe I can find something, sir."

Moving fast, while the clerk went into a back room for the sack, Sammy grabbed the scissors, pulled a length of fuse from the roll, snipped off about three feet, stuffed it in his pocket and put the scissors back on the cutting table.

Just as the clerk came back, he noticed a length of unrolled fuse sticking out from the roll where it would be seen. Sooner or later the clerk would notice it, too, and wonder how it had come unrolled. What to do about it? Sammy worried it over, then had an idea.

"I hope you don't mind if I pull my boot off in here. There's a rock or something in it, and I've got to dump it out right now."

The clerk was busy totaling figures. He glanced up and said, "No, that'll be all right."

Sammy bent over to pull his right boot off, and quickly wrapped the length of fuse tightly around the roll. When he straightened up the clerk was still adding.

He was relieved to see her watching from the lobby. He went in and told her in a low voice that he had the fuse. She got between him and the clerk, took a candle from her pocketbook and handed it to him.

"First thing in the morning, then," he said aloud.

"Yes. Until then." She kissed him on the cheek again. His face tingled deliciously again.

At their camp, he built a small fire and held the can-

dle over it on a stick while Lighthorse located a fairly
flat piece of granite. When the wax was softened,
Lighthorse rolled it out flat with the palms of his hands.
He poured a pile of black gunpowder in the center, put
the end of the fuse inside a percussion cap, and crimped
the sleeve of the cap with his teeth.

"You could lose some teeth that way," Sammy said.

"Unh. Make 'em bomb. Heap big bang."

Then, while the wax was still soft, he rolled it into
a small ball. Sammy quipped, "I hope it doesn't go bang
while we're packing it around. Those percussion caps
won't stand for much jostling."

"It takes a spark or a snap to set 'em off. I played
with one once, and a spark will do it."

"Fact is, I'm not sure we need the cap. The old-time
flint-lock rifles set the powder off with a spark and
nothing else."

"Yeah. Most of the time. This is a sure shot."

"Then we've got a sure-nuff little bomb."

They lay awake most of the night, talking in low
tones, going over their plans. "California is a long ways.
We'll have to go horseback, most of the way anyhow.
According to the only map I've seen, we can ride back
to Albuquerque and go straight west from there. Stay
to hell away from Socorro. We might have to cross some
desert, but not as much as we would if we took a southern route. Mrs. Wilcox said a railroad runs from Denver
to Cheyenne in Wyoming Territory, and we can ride the
rail cars from there all the way to California, but I don't
know how folks in Denver and Cheyenne feel about
Indians."

"No use taking a chance. People have walked to California, you know. Drove oxen and walked. That's what

the schoolteacher said. You say Mrs. Wilcox is gonna take a stage to somewhere in Texas and go by railroad from there?"

"That's what she said. After being robbed east of Albuquerque she's a little leery of traveling by stage, but she can't travel horseback alone."

"I read in an Albuquerque newspaper once that some hardcases are robbing trains, too. Back in Missouri and Kansas. I wonder if California is any better."

"Probably just as many thieves and cutthroats out there. But at least folks there are used to rubbing elbows with different races of people."

"That's the only reason I want to go out there."

Sammy was silent a moment; then he swore, "Goddammit. It just ain't right. I wish there was some way of telling these people how you've risked your life many times to track down the Apaches, to save their hides. Hell, you and the other scouts were always in the lead when we went Apache hunting. You were the first to get shot at. These damn people ought to know about that."

Lighthorse yawned and pulled his blanket up to his chin. "Well, if you can find a way to tell 'em, you tell 'em. Me? All I can say is piss on 'em."

She was ready, saddlebags stuffed, wearing her divided skirt and plain shirtwaist. Her hat was new. It sported a wide brim and a round crown with a plaited string running from the inside down under her throat to hold it on. A throatlatch, some folks called it. A stampede string, cowboys called it. "I told Old Nosy I'm going to Fort Bayard to visit my husband's grave. I said

I'll be back, but I don't know when. I told him you were going to accompany me."

"Lighthorse is on his way. Let's go."

They rode out of Silver City, going east on the wagon road, but as soon as they were out of sight they doubled back northwest, staying in the hills. On the way, Sammy again voiced his complaint about the way Lighthorse was treated by the people he'd risked his life to save.

She agreed. "It is terribly unfair. Lighthorse is really a very handsome young man. In St. Louis the women would be fascinated with him. A real live Indian from the Southwest. Handsome, well-spoken. He'd be very popular, and he'd enjoy life. You would, too, Sammy. You ought to go to St. Louis with me."

Just the thought of traveling with the beautiful Mrs. Wilcox, maybe even sleeping with her, sent a delicious chill through his body. Would she sleep with him?

Naw. Forget it. Besides, he couldn't abandon his partner, not now. Neither he nor Lighthorse expected to be partners for life; but he couldn't just leave him in Albuquerque, and Lighthorse wouldn't want to travel to some eastern city and be pointed at and whispered about.

It sure was a nice thought, though.

While they were riding northwest, clouds were gathering over the high peaks to the west. The clouds were puffy white at first, but as the day wore on they turned dark and started drifting east. Sammy and the woman met Lighthorse before sundown in the timbered draw north of the Packrat mill. They off-saddled and let their horses graze and rest while they ate ginger snaps and cured ham. A light rain began falling.

Sammy grumbled, "Just what we need."

Looking at the sky, Lighthorse said, "Maybe it won't amount to much."

At dark, they saddled up and tied the horses to trees. Using matches, they warmed their wax bomb enough to soften it. First, they looked it over carefully to be sure the flame wouldn't touch the powder. The clouds drifted on, taking the rain with them. A half-moon showed itself, dimly lighting the woods around them.

"I feel the way I used to feel when we were about to tangle with a bunch of renegade Chiricahuas," Sammy said. "Yeah," Lighthorse said, "I think I'd rather shoot it out with old Victorio than this."

Mrs. Wilcox whispered, "I'm just plain scared." She took a deep breath and let it out with a long sigh. "Well, at least it has stopped raining." She took a deep breath again, and said, "It's time for me to go into my act."

"What are you gonna do?" Sammy asked.

"You'll know when it's time for you to act." She left, walking east.

The partners watched her in the light of the half-moon until she was out of sight; then Lighthorse said, "Whatever her plan is, I hope to hell it works."

"If it doesn't, this whole damn thing is all for nothing. I'm not gonna rob anybody at gunpoint."

They moved quietly to where they could see the mill office and its dimly lighted dirty window. Sammy took the extra gunnysack Lighthorse had brought and tied it over one shoulder. A cigarette glowed in front of the office door. They waited. Lighthorse held the small bomb in his hand, his body heat keeping the wax pliable.

"Whatever she's gonna do, I wish she'd do it," Sammy whispered.

"You were right. This is like waiting for the Apaches to attack."

"Come on, lady."

That was when they heard a woman scream. A terrible, blood-chilling, long drawn-out scream.

"Good gawd, she's in trouble."

"No, no," Lighthorse said. "Look."

The office door opened and a man ran out, leaving the door open. He said something to the guard outside. Both drew their pistols, glanced in all directions, and tried to figure out where the scream had come from. The woman screamed again. One of the guards pointed down the road toward Buckhorn. Sammy and Lighthorse looked in the direction he was pointing. They saw her.

Sammy's jaw dropped open in disbelief. Lighthorse muttered, "God, oh, God."

She was naked.

Twenty-six

At first glance the woman looked to be completely naked, but she was wearing underpants. Thin, lacy, transparent. Light slippers on her feet. Beautiful. A beautiful nymph in the woods. She screamed and held her hands over her eyes as if she'd seen something horrible. The two guards ran down the road at her.

Lighthorse said, "She's done her job. Let's go do ours."

There was no use creeping up to the office door. Inside, they shut the door out of habit and to muffle the sound of an explosion. The office was sparsely furnished, with a big scarred desk, one padded spring chair behind the desk, two wooden chairs in front of it, a wooden filing cabinet, two open bookcases holding stacks of papers instead of books, a whiskey bottle one-third full, two coal oil lamps, and a big iron safe.

While Sammy watched, Lighthorse stepped quickly to the safe, bent over and looked closely at the keyhole. He said, "I'll bet he carries the key on a chain around his neck. The key that'll fit this is too big to carry in his pocket."

Nervously, Sammy asked, "Will the damn bomb fit?"

"Unh." Lighthorse pushed the soft wax into the keyhole, leaving the fuse outside. Satisfied that he had the keyhole filled, he struck a match on the safe door, glanced at Sammy, and lit the fuse. It sizzled.

"Take cover," Lighthorse said. "There's gonna be a boom." Sammy squatted behind the desk. Lighthorse joined him.

The explosion shook the office door open, blew the glass out of the one window and blew out the lamps. Black smoke shot out of the keyhole. Both Sammy and Lighthorse jumped up and tried the safe door. It wouldn't budge.

"Goddam, goddam," Sammy said nervously. While Lighthorse lighted one of the lamps, he reached for his pocket knife, then remembered he'd given it to the woman. "Shit, goddam."

Holding the lamp close, Lighthorse jerked his belt knife out of its holster and stuck it in the keyhole, twisted it. "Something moved," he said. "Everything is busted in there." He grabbed the door handle, turned it down and pulled. The door opened.

"The sack. Did you bring the gunnysack?" Lighthorse asked.

"Right here," Sammy said.

They had to fan the smoke away with their hands to see inside the safe. Then Lighthorse exclaimed, "God, oh, God, look at this."

Four stacks of money, U.S. greenbacks, filled a shelf. Canvas bags of rocks sat on the floor. While Sammy hastily crammed the paper money into the gunnysack, Lighthorse opened one of the bags. "Gold," he said, almost reverently. "It's got to be pure gold."

"Leave it." With all the paper money in the gunnysack, Sammy said, "Let's haul our asses out of here. Those guards must have heard the blast."

"I hate to leave this gold. Look. Pokes of dust. Gold dust."

"Let's go."

"You're right."

Lighthorse set the lamp on the desk, and bolted through the door. Sammy was right behind him. They ran, not trying to muffle their footsteps, until they were among the trees, in black shadows. There they stopped and looked back.

Sammy said, "I don't see anybody. Do you?"

"Nope, but they were bound to have heard the racket."

"Goddam," Sammy said, "you don't reckon they caught her?"

"If they did, they won't turn her loose for a while."

"I don't want that to happen. No sir."

"Let's find the horses and get ready to ride."

The three horses, two bay geldings and a sorrel mare, snorted when they approached, but didn't pull back. The partners untied all three and, holding the reins, waited.

"Surely," Sammy said, "she had a spot picked out to run to and hide."

"She's not dumb, that woman. You can bet she had it planned right down to a gnat's ass."

"This plan has worked too good so far. Something has to go wrong."

"Something already did."

"What?"

"The rain. The ground is so soft now a school kid could follow our tracks."

"Yeah, we might as well paint signs on the trees."

"Somebody's coming.

With shallow breaths, they waited, guns in their hands, straining their eyes to see in the dark. They saw her before she saw them. She was walking fast but not running, and she started to pass them on the north. "Over here," Sammy whispered. She turned and came up, breathing heavily.

"I'm not sure I got all the buttons done, but I think I'm ready to ride. Did you get the money?"

"Yeah. Stacks of it. Did you hear the explosion?"

"No. I was hiding in some brush. I let them chase me as far as I safely could before I ducked into my hidey hole. All I could hear was them running around looking for me. And my heart beating."

Lighthorse whispered, "We've got to go."

She said, "I know you're planning to go north from here while I find my way back to Silver City. Give me my share, and I'll be on my way."

"We can't count this here in the dark. We don't dare strike a match or anything."

"You're right. I didn't have everything planned after all. Well, just give me what feels like a third."

Lighthorse said, "We're gonna have to change our plans."

"Yeah," Sammy said. "We didn't plan on rain making the ground so soft. If we went north from here, they'd be right on our tails."

Mounting, Lighthorse said, "The first thing we've got to do is get away from here. Follow me."

Sammy and the woman mounted and followed him, Sammy hanging on to the gunnysack of money, Lighthorse carrying the sack of grub. "Shhh," Lighthorse cautioned. Sammy whispered, "I wish we could muffle the sound of hoofbeats."

The Indian led them wide around the town of Buckhorn, through the darkest shadows, Sammy in the middle and the woman in the rear. Once, when a tree limb hit Sammy in the face, he reined up and whispered, "Watch out for the limbs. Hold your arm in front of your face." He heard her grunt as she rode into the limb, but he didn't hear her fall.

East of the town now, Lighthorse turned his horse south until they came to the wagon road leading to Silver City. In a low tone, he said, "It doesn't matter now as long as nobody see us."

Sammy agreed. "We're making tracks no matter which way we go."

"If we're lucky," Lighthorse said, "somebody will come along with a four-up and a wagon and cover our tracks."

Turning in his saddle, Sammy asked, "How're you doing, Mrs. Wilcox?"

"I'm all right. Lighthorse, where are we going from here? We can't ride right into Silver City."

"No. We'll go around Silver City, and come out on the road going east. Maybe there'll be enough moonlight that we can count the money."

"This is better for you than our first plan," Sammy said to the woman. "You won't have to ride so far alone to get back to your hotel."

"Yes, there's that."

Again they rode around a town in the dark, this time a bigger town, and the traveling was over rough, rocky ground, in and out of gulches and arroyos. But they'd been over this ground before, and Lighthorse led them to the east side of Silver City and back to the road. There they stopped, dismounted and tried to count the money in the light of the half-moon.

"This is not the best way to do this," Sammy said. "I can't tell a twenty-dollar bill from a one."

She said, "We'll just have to do the best we can."

"Somebody's gonna get cheated."

"We can't stand here all night," Lighthorse said.

"All right," the woman said, "I just changed my plan, too."

"How's that?" Sammy asked.

"I'm going north with you."

Sammy sputtered, "But . . . but . . ."

"That will simplify everything. We can count the money in the daylight, and I won't have to make up a lie about why I came back to the hotel at four or five o'clock in the morning. That's something else I didn't plan on."

"But, well . . ."

"Besides, this money is safer with you two than it would be on a stagecoach."

Lighthorse said, "If that's the way it is, that's the way it is. Get on your horses and let's go."

They stayed on the road until they came to a brushy arroyo, then turned north and pushed through the brush. "Maybe," Lighthorse said, "they won't see where we quit the road."

"Maybe," the woman said, "they'll think we went on east and then southeast to Deming."

"That's more maybes than I like," Lighthorse said.

Sammy was quiet, thinking. He was thinking about how Mrs. Wilcox had looked back there, naked. Or nearly so. He'd never seen anything as beautiful, or as exciting. Her breasts, perfectly formed, her narrow waist, her rounded, tapered thighs. Her buttocks when she had turned and run. Just picturing her again in his mind made his mouth dry, his hands shaky. He felt weak all over as instinctive desire coursed through his body.

He couldn't help groaning out loud, "Ohhh, lordy."

"Is something wrong, Sammy?" she asked.

Good God, if she only knew. But he answered, "No. Nothing."

Silently, they rode in the night, through the woods, across clearings, across wide draws and narrow arroyos. The two partners, carrying gunnysacks, couldn't fend off the tree limbs with their forearms and had to depend on their hat brims to protect their faces. The green conifer needles were soft, but the dead brown ones were prickly.

At the first sign of daylight, Lighthorse stopped. "I don't know if anyone will be on our trail, but even if there is, we have to let these animals rest and graze. If we don't, we're gonna be afoot, and it's a long ways to Albuquerque."

"I don't think I'm capable of walking that far," the woman said.

They off-saddled in a grassy draw and let their horses graze on the blue grama and wheatgrass. But before they rested themselves they had to count the money. Sammy dumped the money onto an open saddle blanket, and, on their knees, they counted.

Finally, Mrs. Wilcox said, "I've got a thousand and four hundred dollars in this pile." Sammy continued counting, then said, "There's nine hundred and ten here." It took Lighthorse longer to count his pile, but finally he looked up and grinned. "Two thousand, two hundred and ninety."

The woman frowned in concentration. "That totals, um, four thousand, six hundred dollars."

Sammy let out a low whistle. Lighthorse continued smiling. The woman frowned again. "Let's see, divided by three, that's, um, one thousand, five hundred, and um, thirty-three dollars."

Sammy whistled again. "That's more than a soldier gets in over three years."

"Shall we divide it now?" the woman asked.

"If you want to," Sammy said. "My saddlebags are stuffed full, though, and I can't carry that much in my pockets. How about you all?"

"I'm in the same condition," the woman said. "Perhaps later, after we consume some of what we're carrying in our saddlebags."

Lighthorse said, "Whatever pleases you all suits me."

After three hours' rest, they saddled up and rode on. Neither the humans nor animals had rested enough, but the humans wanted to get as far north as they could as fast as they could. Every thirty minutes or so, Lighthorse dropped back, dismounted and studied the country behind them. Each time he shook his head when he rejoined them. They stayed west of Fort Bayard and hoped they wouldn't see any army patrols.

At dusk, they stopped on the bank of a small stream. Horses unsaddled and grazing, they ate a cold meal. Lighthorse walked back to where he could see for some distance and stayed there until dark. By sunup the next day they were riding again. Soon they crossed Diamond Creek and were headed into the Elk Mountains.

On the third day they had to make a decision. Lighthorse said, "These animals of ours ain't holding up too good, Sammy."

"Yeah, I know. They're working too hard climbing these hills, and they're not getting enough feed and rest."

"They weren't in the best of shape when we started on this journey."

"They've lived on grass and rocks too long. But Mrs. Wilcox's mare is doing all right. She's about a thousand pounds bigger than these horses, and she's been eating good hay and grain in the livery pens for a long time. She's also carrying the lightest load."

"What we're gonna have to do," Lighthorse said, "is put more of the load on that mare. These two gunnysacks and some of what's in our saddlebags."

"Is that all right with you, Mrs. Wilcox?"

She dragged a shirtsleeve across her eyes, let out a weary sigh and said, "Whatever you think is best."

They piled groceries on top of money in one of the sacks, trying to even the weight on both sides. Then they tied the tops of the sacks together and hung them across the fork of the woman's saddle. "If this gets uncomfortable, we'll try something else," Sammy said.

"It will be fine."

"How are you holding up?"

She sighed. "I'm tired, of course, but I'm thinking about how wonderful it will be to get to Albuquerque and deposit this money in a bank."

"Two or three more days."

They'd crossed the Plains of San Agustin, ridden around the San Mateo Mountains and were within sight of the Rio Grande when they again met Sheriff Elmer Pogue of Socorro.

Twenty-seven

The woman had excused herself and ridden into a deep arroyo. The men rode on, taking themselves out of sight. Lighthorse said, "I've gotta drain mine, too, or bust a gut."

"If I don't unload in the next few minutes, it's gonna be coming out of my eyes," Sammy said.

They rode on, looking back to be sure they were out of her sight, then got down. "Ahhh," said Lighthorse. "I'm shedding five pounds," said Sammy.

"There's a man over there," Lighthorse said, pointing across a yucca-dotted plain.

"Yeah, and he sees us."

"He's too far away to recognize, but he's coming our way, coming on a high trot."

"Yep, he's double-timing it. Let's go meet 'im, keep 'im from seeing Mrs. Wilcox. Maybe he won't be too curious if he doesn't see her."

"There's only one man. Nothing to be afraid of. But you're right, it might be best if he doesn't see the woman."

Buttoning up hastily, they mounted and rode at a trot to meet the oncoming rider. "Uh-oh," said Lighthorse.

"God damn. Not him."

"Him. I'd recognize his short, thick carcass and the way he sticks his pant legs inside his boots even if he didn't have that badge pinned to his shirt."

"Shit. And these horses are in no shape for a horse race."

"And I don't want to shoot 'im."

"Hell's hooks. Of all the people we could meet, why does it have to be that yahoo."

"Something goes wrong with every plan."

Reining up, they waited, hands away from their guns. Sammy's heart was in his stomach. This was the end of everything. Lighthorse scowled, thinking about that Socorro County jail. Sheriff Elmer Pogue rode up with a six-gun in his hand. He drawled, "Well, if you two don't lead the goddam parade. This is the second time I was lookin' for you, and both times you came right up to me. This is almost like whistlin' for a dog."

Sammy forced a weak grin and tried to joke, but his voice was flat. "Why, Sheriff Pogue, as I live and breathe. Now, why would you be looking for us?" While he said it, his stomach was rapidly turning sour.

"Oh," the sheriff said, returning the grin, "I get lonesome when I ain't got nobody locked up in my jail."

Feeling sick, too, Lighthorse said, "I don't reckon you'll put another pickpocket in with us."

"Is that what happened? That little feller picked my deputy's pocket?"

"He was so smooth we didn't even see 'im do it."

"Well now." The sheriff's face and voice showed he was through with small talk. "S'posin' you two take them peestolas out'n them flap holsters and drop 'em on the ground. And," he barked, "do it right now."

They did as ordered, and two six-guns hit the dirt.

"Now," Sheriff Pogue barked, "get away from 'em."
They reined their horses away. "Not too far, god damn
it." Dismounted, the sheriff picked up the two pistols
and stuck them under his belt. He had to hold them
there with a forearm until he got back on his horse.
"All right, now. You know where to go."

"We've been there before," Sammy grumbled. He
wondered whether the woman had seen what was happening and was staying out of sight, but he didn't dare
look back.

The Socorro County jail was empty until they walked
in. As the iron-barred door clanked shut, Lighthorse
looked at the ceiling. He was surprised to see the cutting
they'd done with a spoon hadn't been touched.

"We're entitled to a trial, you know," Sammy said to
Elmer Pogue's back. The sheriff half-turned. "In due
time, in due time."

Sitting on the bunks, heads in their hands, they were
lost in their own thoughts. Sammy's morale had sunk
so low he felt like quitting. Just stopping his brain and
feeling nothing. Wait for the hangman's noose or a long
prison term. Lighthorse was feeling hopeless, too. He
didn't want to die this way. Not dangling from a rope
and not rotting away in prison. He wished he could be
buried beside his mother and father, up north in the
snowy mountains.

Both men were so numb they didn't move, didn't talk.
When their supper was delivered, they stood and, moving like wooden men, went to the back of the cell as
ordered. They didn't touch their supper.

"Weel now," the sheriff said the next morning. "You

boys should've ate your grub. It ain't all that bad." He turned his head when the office door opened, then said, "Here's breakfast. You boys step back now, against the wall. Behave yourselves and there won't be no trouble."

They stood against the wall while two tin plates of hotcakes with syrup were placed on the floor, this time by a teenaged boy. When the barred door was shut and locked, Elmer Pogue said, "Eat hearty, boys, who knows what the day will bring."

The day brought nothing. The partners did eat, however. They stood against the wall again while the boy picked up their empty plates. "You all behave yourselves; now," the sheriff repeated. "And don't think I didn't notice what you done to the ceiling. Don't try nothin' like that again or I'll have to chain you to your bunks."

"Like a dog on a chain," Lighthorse grouched. "That's what he wants to do to us."

"He's mad because we busted out of his jail once."

"Yeah, but he sure is a happy man now that he's got us back."

"Captured us all by himself, he did, two desperadoes, two cold-blooded killers."

"Bet he's the town hero now."

"Piss on him."

Silently, they sat, lay back on their bunks, sat up, paced the cell, sat. Sammy said, "Wonder if she got away. Old Hound Dog Pogue ain't so smart after all. He doesn't know about her."

"She's a hell of a lot smarter than he is any day. She's smart enough to get herself across the river and on the road to Albuquerque. There's enough traffic on that road that she's probably safe traveling by herself."

"You know what? She's got all the money. She's got everything we risked our asses for. And here we sit."

"Yep, she won't be in Albuquerque a day before she'll have that money in a bank in her name. And she'll be on the next stage out of there."

"She wins again. We lose again."

"Shit."

On the third day the sheriff brought them a pan of water and a straight razor. "You can shave if you want to or you can let your beard grow," he said to Sammy. To Lighthorse, he said, "You Indians don't know how lucky you are you don't have to shave."

It was shortly after breakfast on the fourth day, a breakfast of cold hotcakes and lukewarm coffee, that Sheriff Pogue unlocked the iron-barred door and swung it open. "All right, boys, come on out of there."

"What?" Sammy said, looking up from his bunk.

"Is it trial time?" Lighthorse asked.

"No trial for you boys."

"Well, then, what?" Sammy smelled something suspicious about this. He walked to the open door slowly. "What's going on?"

"You boys've freeloaded off the county long enough. Come on out of there."

Sammy stepped warily through the door and into the sheriff's office. Lighthorse was right behind him. The deputy was there, scowling. He took a double-barreled shotgun from the rack on the wall, broke it open and shoved two shells into the bores, then went outside.

The sheriff said, "All right, come on over here and pick up your stuff. Here's your peestolas."

Now Sammy was convinced that this wasn't what it

was supposed to be. "We're packing guns to the court-house?"

"You ain't goin' to the courthouse."

"Well . . . ?" He knew then. That deputy outside with the shotgun, he was planning to shoot them in the back as soon as they stepped outside. Their plan, the sheriff's and the deputy's, was to claim they were shot when they tried to escape. He glanced at Lighthorse, wondering whether he was also suspicious. Lighthorse's eyes were guarded.

They'd get away with it, too. They'd remind the townspeople that these two had busted out of jail before.

Lighthorse picked up his six-gun. He checked the loads, then buckled on his gunbelt. Sammy believed that was a mistake. That was playing the lawmen's game. He left his belongings on the sheriff's desk.

Fear formed a lump in his throat as he asked, "Why no trial?"

"No need for a trial."

Sammy swallowed a lump in his throat and tried to force down the fear. He locked his gaze onto the sheriff's face. "If you intend to shoot us in the back, you can do it right in here. While I'm not armed."

Eyes narrowed now, Sheriff Pogue said, "What the Sam Hill're you talkin' about?"

"I'm talking about that deputy out there with a shotgun, just waiting for us."

Lighthorse quickly unbuckled his gunbelt and put it back on the sheriff's desk. "If that's your scheme, you'll have to shoot me while I'm unarmed and looking at you."

"What in hell're you . . . ? Oh." Sheriff Pogue's eyes suddenly widened. "I get it. You think . . . Naw. My deputy is plumb over by the river now. He went over there to try to settle a dispute between two Mexicans. He ain't gonna shoot nobody. Them Mexicans see that big gun, they'll get peaceable right fast. They'll find something to agree on."

"Then what's this all about?" Sammy demanded.

Now Elmer Pogue was grinning. "Simmer down, boys. Don't get your dander up. Let me show you something." He opened a desk drawer and took out a wanted poster and a letter-sized envelope with an address scrawled on it. "Read this first." He handed the poster to Sammy.

Standing close together, the partners read: "WANTED FOR MURDER." Under that was a name: "THOMAS HAWLEY." Under that in smaller print: "Dead or Alive. If seen, notify Sheriff Peterson Goddard, Potter County, Texas, or any U.S. marshal or deputy marshal." Under that was the message, "Extremely Dangerous."

The partners exchanged glances; then Lighthorse asked, "Who is Thomas Hawley?"

"I forgot you're a civilized Indian and can read. Here." The sheriff handed Lighthorse the envelope. "Read this."

Lighthorse took out a folded sheet of ruled paper, and the partners read:

"To Sheriff Elmer Pogue—Socorro County, Ter. of New Mexico. I am sure now that we can close the case on Thomas Hawley. The description you wrote of the deceased in your county fits perfectly with the description we have of the suspect. There is no doubt that he was the man who shot and killed a grocery clerk and robbed the cash box. When we arrested him we took notice of all identifying marks. We thank you for taking notice of the same before burying the deceased. The knife scar across his left side and the two missing front teeth you described in your last letter made the identification positive. The other deceased in your jurisdiction as described in your letter fits the description of the man we believe helped Thomas Hawley escape from the Amarillo jail. We in all of north Texas are in your debt for bringing to an end the career of this dangerous killer."

The letter was signed, "Sheriff Grant Beazley."

Dumbfounded, Lighthorse asked, "Are you saying one of the men we shot up there in the Elks was this Thomas Hawley?"

"Yep." The sheriff dropped into his spring-back chair. "No doubt about it. He gave a bogus name to his boss at the Packrat mill, but that's him. I suspicioned as much when I got that there wanted flyer in the mail. Mail delivery is almighty slow in these parts, and Sheriff Beazley and me, we had to write back and forth several times to get it all straightened out. That there letter came in yesterday's mail. I showed it to the prosecutor last night, and him and me talked it over last night, and again this mornin'. He says no jury would convict you two."

After another exchange of glances, Sammy said, "Come to think of it, I remember somebody saying that the man the gold was stolen from liked to hire hardcases."

"Yep." The sheriff leaned back in his chair. "That's what I learned, too. Harrels is the man's name. I doubt if he knew he was hirin' Thomas Hawley, but his reputation ain't none to clean either."

Still not convinced, Sammy asked, "Then we really are free to go?"

"Yep. The prosecutor says the only crime he can stick you with is jailbreak, but he thinks a jury would find you innocent of that, too, considerin' you was jailed for a crime you didn't do. Trials cost money, and if the prosecutor lost, he'd be laughed at. Or cussed at."

"Well"—Sammy rubbed the back of his neck and grinned—"I'll be damned."

"Pick up your stuff and git. You've got enough money there to bail your horses out of hock at the livery barn, and not much else, but you're free men."

As they followed a wagon road north, paralleling the Rio Grande, the partners had mixed feelings. Lighthorse said, "No matter what, we're not wanted by the law anymore, and that makes me feel like I just dumped a back-breaking load."

"Yeah, but we're damn near broke. I've got enough spendulics to pay for a night in a hotel and buy a couple of meals, and that's all. But I'm so damned glad to be out of jail and right with the law that I ain't gonna worry about anything else for a while."

"I was thinking, when we were sitting in jail, about a map I saw once that showed a range of high mountains we'd have to cross in California. The Sierra somethingorother. And I remember reading about a bunch of folks that was trapped in deep snow in those mountains. They got so hungry they ate their own dead. I don't think I want to try to cross those mountains in the winter."

"Come to think of it, I remember seeing that map,"

Sammy said. "And if we started out now, it would be winter when we got there."

"We don't have to quit the country now anyway."

They camped on the west bank of the river south of Belen. They had some jerky and dried fruit to munch on, but no pot to cook anything in. Just the same, Sammy broke up a dead cottonwood limb and built a small fire. A man and wife with two young children camped about two hundred yards south of them. They were traveling in a wagon pulled by two horses.

"Probably going up to Albuquerque to hunt for a job," Sammy mused.

"Probably. That coffee they're cooking sure smells good."

"I smell meat frying, too."

"Oh, well, might as well forget it."

"Might as well."

In Albuquerque, they paid for a room in the Casa Grande Hotel, a room with one narrow bed, a wash-stand, a washbasin, a cracked mirror and nails in the wall to hang their clothes on.

"We can eat supper in a cafe tonight or breakfast in the morning," Sammy said. "Pick one."

Sitting on the bed, running his fingers through his black hair, Lighthorse said, "We've still got some jerky and apples in those saddlebags. That will do for supper. In the morning maybe we can pay for some hot hotcakes and bacon and coffee."

After blowing out the lamp and crawling between muslin sheets, Sammy tried to joke, "Know something? If we'd stayed in that jail much longer, we'd have been so skinny we wouldn't have had enough weight to hang."

Chuckling dryly, Lighthorse said, "They'd have had to tie rocks to our feet."

At breakfast in a cafe across the street from the plaza, the partners cleaned every crumb from their plates and drained every drop from their coffee cups. Outside, they sat on a wooden bench in the plaza and talked. They decided they'd have to go separate ways. Lighthorse said he knew he'd have to go back to work for the U.S. Army sooner or later, and it might as well be sooner.

"Colonel Johnstone told me when I left Fort Union I'd have a job there if I wanted to come back." Snorting, he added, "He knew I'd be back. He knew I had no choice."

"You scouts get a better deal than us dogface soldiers. You get the same pay, and you don't have to snap to attention and salute every time an officer comes around. You don't have to Sir anybody, and you don't have to drill, drill, goddam drill."

"That's so."

"I can get a job, but I'll starve before I get my first pay. Or, maybe I can get a job on a ranch where I'll get a bunk and grub. I'm no cowboy; but I know horses, and I sure as hell know how to shovel shit."

"There's probably more work on a ranch than chasing cows, anyway."

"I guess that's what I'll do. I wish I knew a trade to work at. I spent so much time in the army, I don't know how to make a living in the civilian world."

"What kind of trade?"

"Know what I'd like to do? I'd like to work with leather, build saddles and make harnesses. I like to handle leather. I like the smell and feel of it."

"How do you go about learning a trade like that?"

"I don't know. Learn from somebody, I reckon."

After a long moment of silence, Lighthorse said, "It's a good thing we paid ahead for a night for our horses. We'd better go get 'em before we get stuck for another day and night."

Sammy reached into his pocket for what change he had left, counted it twice. "I've got twenty-four cents. What have you got?"

"Thirty-seven cents. I already counted it."

"I'll have to camp out somewhere until I land a job on a ranch."

"I'll camp with you until you do; then I'll head on up to Fort Union."

"Sure could use a bath and some clean clothes. Maybe I can find a place in the river."

Standing, Lighthorse said, "Well, let's go find a place."

The partners had picked up their saddlebags and blanket rolls and were ready to leave their hotel room when there came a knock on the door. The hotel clerk stood there.

"Someone out in the lobby wants to see you," he said.

"Who?" Suddenly, Sammy was wary. The clerk only shrugged, turned and left.

"Goddam. You don't reckon that sheriff at Socorro thought of something else?"

Shaking his head sadly, a worry wrinkle on his forehead, Lighthorse said, "I don't know. We can't run, so I guess we'll have to go and see."

Twenty-eight

With resignation, prepared for bad news, the partners left the hotel room, walked down a short hall to the small lobby—and stopped suddenly. For a moment, neither was able to speak.

"Hello, Sammy, Lighthorse. You seem surprised to see me."

"Well, uh," Sammy stuttered, "fact is . . . we, uh . . ."

Lighthorse finished for him, "We didn't expect to see you."

"We thought you'd be on your way to St. Louis."

"No, not yet. As a matter of fact, I have engaged an attorney to represent you. He is ready to take the stagecoach to Socorro today. I, uh, I thought I saw you two come in here just now. I'm just as surprised as you are. What happened? How . . . ?"

She was wearing a new pink dress, belted in the middle, with white lace and big white buttons. Her feet were encased in new shoes with black buttons to her ankles.

Sammy was still flabbergasted. He shook his head. "Boy, oh, boy, uh, let's go somewhere and talk."

"Yes. This is very interesting. How about the plaza?"

They walked the half block and across the street to the plaza, then sat on the bench the two partners had just vacated. She turned her face and knees toward them. "I saw the sheriff from Socorro pick up your guns, and I saw you ride away. I thought you were in such serious trouble that you needed an attorney."

Relief was evident on Sammy's face. "We thought we were as good as hung. Or in prison. But . . . Lighthorse, you tell her."

Lighthorse told her. She put a palm to her forehead and exclaimed, "I should have known that all along. Of course. We, my late husband and I, knew Mr. Harrels hired toughs to work for him and help him steal claims. And that's not all. The news from Silver City is definitely in our favor."

"What news?"

"I have a copy of a newspaper from Silver City in my room at the hotel. You should read it for yourselves. Wait right here and I'll go get it." She stood and walked with rapid steps across the street to the Coronado Hotel.

"Any idea what she's talking about?" Lighthorse asked.

"No, but she said it's good news. I'll tell you, just seeing her again is good news."

"She didn't say anything about the money."

"If it has been stolen or anything, she'd have said so. Now that we've got her, we've got the money."

"Here she comes back."

She was smiling, handing the newspaper to Sammy. "This came in on last night's stage from the east. It was printed just a day after we left Silver City, but it took this long to arrive here by mail."

The one-column headline in big, bold print read, "MILL OWNER MURDERED."

A subhead under that read, "Found Shot In Office of Packrat Mill."

Another subhead under that read, "Robbery Believed The Motive."

The two partners read the headlines and looked at each other. "We didn't shoot anybody," Lighthorse said. "We didn't even see anybody."

"Read on," the woman said, smiling.

With their heads together, the partners read the story:

"Mr. Jason Harrels, owner of the Packrat Mine & Milling Works, was found in his office with a bullet in his heart late Thursday morning, and the safe in the office had been rifled.

"Sheriff Paul Benson believes he was the victim of a robbery murder. He is looking for two men who had been hired to guard the office and safe at night. The sheriff said the safe had been blown open with blasting powder, and surmised the two guards were in the process of stealing its contents when Mr. Harrels surprised them in the act.

"The two guards, identified as Joseph Milner and William Teller, were nowhere to be found. Two horses were also missing from the company's freight yard and corral behind the mill. Fresh horse tracks led from the office westward, and Sheriff Benson believes the killers fled in that direction. A heavily armed posse of men from Silver City was organized; but Sheriff Benson said the fugitives are mounted on two of several well-bred horses which Mr. Harrels kept in his corral, and he believes they had a head start of approximately twelve hours.

"Missing from the safe is a large amount of cash and several bags of gold dust. A brick of refined gold is also missing. Several heavy sacks of high-grade gold ore were left behind. Sheriff Benson believes they were not taken because of their weight. At this writing, the sheriff and five townsmen are in pursuit of the murderers.

"The body of Mr. Harrels was discovered at mid-morning Thursday by a mine superintendent, who immediately notified the sheriff."

Sammy put the paper down and, flabbergasted for the second time that morning, looked at his partner. "Well, if that don't beat all."

"It sure does. What do you make of all this, Mrs. Wilcox?"

Still smiling, she said, "It's definitely good news. What obviously happened is the two guards went back to the office, found the safe wide open, knew they were going to be fired, and decided to take what they could and run. It was Mr. Harrels' misfortune to step into his office at that time. I don't know why he went to his office at night, but for some reason he did."

Lighthorse added, "And the sheriff and his posse went chasing after those two yahoos."

"They don't know about us," the woman said.

"Yeah, but . . ." Sammy shrugged. "You know me, always the worrier. What if the sheriff catches 'em alive and they tell the whole story?"

"They won't be believed," the woman said. "Would you believe them?"

Lighthorse said, "Our trail was cold by the time the sheriff caught 'em or gave up. And if those two ain't caught, or if they're shot to death, well . . ." He, too, shrugged.

"Now," the woman said, "about our money. I put it in the Coronado's safe. It's still in a burlap bag, and I know the desk clerk was curious as to why I'd put a burlap bag in the hotel's safe. The German who was manager is no longer there, and a man who looks to be half-Mexican has taken his place. Well, sure enough, when I checked on it, the bag had been opened."

"Think he took some of it?" Sammy asked.

"I don't know, but I doubt it. If he did and I complained, he would be suspect. However, there have been two tough-looking men watching me. They're always in the lobby or standing in the street just outside the hotel, and they have been following me. As a matter of fact, there they are now, over there across the street. See them?"

They were easy to spot, the two who leaned against a brick building and pretended they were paying no attention to anything in particular. Both wore baggy brown duck pants, blue chambray work shirts, and shapeless fedora hats. They also wore six-guns in holsters low on their right hips.

"They've been following you?" Lighthorse asked.

"Yes. I think they're waiting for me to walk out of the hotel with that burlap bag. I think they want to rob me."

"Right out here on the street in broad daylight?"

"They could grab the bag and run. There are any number of narrow, crooked streets and shacks they could disappear into. They could drag me into an alley and club me over the head or stab me and run."

"There's no way you can walk out of the hotel with that much money without being seen."

"That's true, no matter what I carry it in."

Sammy said, "We've got to put it in a bank. We ought to do that right now."

Lighthorse stood. "All right, let's get it done."

The woman and Sammy stood, too. "I'm certainly glad you gentlemen are here. I was worried about carrying that money by myself. What we can do is divide it in my room, and you can accompany me to a bank. You can do whatever you wish with your share."

"Mine is going into a bank, too. But maybe not the same bank."

"Mine, too," Lighthorse said.

The desk clerk opened the safe and handed over the gunnysack, but he objected to the men accompanying the woman to her room. Mrs. Wilcox was in no mood for argument. "We are going to my room to conduct some private business. Understand?"

The clerk gulped and said, *"Si."*

With a third of their loot counted out, the woman produced a new leather satchel and stuffed the greenbacks inside. The men had nothing but the gunnysack to carry their share in, so they watched the desk clerk put it back in the safe. "We will reclaim it in a very short time," the woman told the clerk.

As they started to leave the hotel, Lighthorse called them back. Whispering, he said, "I see 'em out there. They'll know as soon as they spot that satchel, and they'll be right behind you, watching for a chance. What I think I'll do is hang back. If they follow you, I'll follow them. I've got the flap unbuttoned on my gun holster so I'll be ready."

"Good strategy," Sammy said. "With you on their flank maybe they won't try anything."

"I've chosen the Central Bank of Albuquerque," Mrs. Wilcox said. "It seems to be the biggest bank in the city, and probably the most reliable. But it is a block from the plaza."

"All right, you two go ahead. I'll be behind you."

As they walked across the plaza, crossed the street and turned down a side street, Sammy whispered, "I hear their footsteps. Don't look back. Let's just keep walking." They walked. Out of the corner of his eye, Sammy saw a sign painted on the window of a narrow, one-story building that stood between two two-story buildings. The sign read, "Sandia Saddles & Harness." Another, small sign was printed on a square of cardboard just inside a small windowpane. It read, "Apprentice Wanted."

It caught his attention, and he had to stop and try to look through the window. That was when quick footsteps came up behind them and a gun was poked into the middle of his back.

A low, hard voice said, "Get over there. Get over there between them houses and do it fast or I'll kill you right here."

Sammy heard the woman suck in her breath. He swore, "What the goddam hell is going on?"

"Shut up. And don't look at us."

Silently, Sammy cursed himself. He'd just had to stupidly stop and make it easy for them. How stupid could anyone get? He thought he ought to be shot. He started to turn his head, and the gun barrel jabbed him harder.

"I said don't look at us. Now move god damn it. And don't make a sound, neither of you. My finger is already squeezin' this trigger."

With wooden steps, Sammy turned into the narrow space between the saddle shop and a haberdashery. The woman was shoved so hard she almost went sprawling, but managed to regain her balance. The satchel was jerked from her hand. Sammy's six-gun was pulled from its holster.

"On your bellies. Facedown in them weeds. Move, god damn it. And don't look up for a long time."

Then Lighthorse barked, "Halt. Stand right still. I can drop you both in your tracks."

Sammy looked back then. It was the two men they'd spotted near the hotel. Their eyes were rolling around in their sockets as they tried to decide whether they wanted to turn and shoot.

"Don't try it," Sammy warned. "He's got you dead to rights."

"Sammy, get their guns."

The first one didn't want to let go of his gun until Lighthorse barked, "One wrong move and you're dead." Sammy was able to take both their guns then.

The woman, shaken, voice wavering, asked, "What should we do with them?"

Sammy's mind raced. They couldn't turn them over to the police. The police would ask questions about the money. They couldn't just let them go either. Sammy holstered his own pistol, then viciously swung one of the other guns up in an arc that ended against one gunsel's nose. Bone crunched and blood spurted. The man fell hard onto the seat of his pants, holding his face in both hands. The other man was knocked to his knees with a blow from Lighthorse's gun.

"All right," Lighthorse drawled, "stick their pistols inside that bag and let's go to the bank."

Twenty-nine

The partners waited on the plank walk outside the bank while the woman opened an account. Lighthorse said, "I know she's smart enough not to let anybody see those pistols when she takes the money out of her bag."

"Don't worry about her," Sammy said.

While they waited, Sammy went back up the street and noted with satisfaction that the two gunsels were gone. A spot of blood covered some weeds where they had been. Then he looked through the dirty window of the saddle and harness shop. He could see a man inside, but not much else.

The woman came out of the bank smiling.

"I had to keep enough cash for traveling expenses, but the rest is safe and sound. As soon as I get to St. Louis I'll start the process of having it transferred to a St. Louis bank."

Their next stop was at the bottom of a flight of wooden stairs that climbed the side of a two-story stone building across the plaza. Again Sammy and Lighthorse waited. When she came down, she said, "I told him his legal services were not needed after all. What I had to pay him was nominal."

They walked her back to her hotel, where they collected the gunnysack and walked, swinging the sack casually, to their room. Within two hours both young men had opened accounts in separate banks. When the cashier at Sammy's chosen bank asked where he got so much money, Sammy answered, "I was in the army a long time. I saved." Lighthorse's answer was, "I worked for the U.S. Army a long time, and there ain't much an Indian can spend money on."

Meeting in the plaza, Lighthorse mused, "Between the three of us we've got money in every bank in this town. They can't all go broke."

They went shopping. In another two hours they had fresh haircuts and baths and were wearing new clothes. Rubbing his hand over the top of his head, Sammy said, "I feel like a peeled onion."

Lighthorse quipped, "I had to buy a new hat. My old one doesn't fit anymore."

"I'd throw my old clothes in the river, but they'd poison the water for a hundred miles downstream."

"She said she wants us to have supper together. She's been here long enough to know where the best restaurant is."

Supper was good. Fresh-butchered beef, medium rare, mashed potatoes and milk gravy, corn on the cob, beans cooked as only the Mexicans knew how to cook them, and peach pie.

Mrs. Wilcox chatted gaily while the men ate their fill. Then, when the men leaned back in their chairs and patted their stomachs, she asked, "What do you think now? Was it worth it?"

"Yes," Lighthorse said, thoughtfully. "Now that it's

all over, now that the smoke has cleared, I believe it was worth it."

Sammy said, "I wouldn't do it again for anything in the world, but yes, I'm glad we did it once. How about you, Mrs. Wilcox? You sure did your share, and you put up with some long horseback trips."

She didn't answer immediately, and when she spoke she was dead serious. "Before Henry was cheated out of his mining claim, something he—we—had worked long and hard for, I wouldn't have considered such a thing. But the more I thought about it, the angrier I became. I truly believe there are times when a body is justified in going outside the law."

"Uh-huh," Sammy said. Lighthorse nodded in agreement.

"Well," she said, smiling again, "what are your plans for the future?"

Lighthorse smiled and said, "There's a little gal down at Fort Bayard who doesn't know it yet, but she's gonna be Mrs. Lighthorse Jones. I'm gonna get my job back at Fort Union, then go break the news to her."

"Why, that's wonderful, Lighthorse. That's really wonderful."

"Some day," Lighthorse continued, "the Indian wars will be over, and we can buy a few acres somewhere and raise some goats and chickens and vegetables. And kids."

Sammy chuckled, "It will happen, pardner, just the way you want it. Old Victorio and Geronimo will have to surrender to a superior force. It won't be long now."

"And you, Sammy, what are your plans?"

Slowly, Sammy's smile vanished, and a frown creased his forehead. "I don't know yet. I just don't know."

Mrs. Wilcox went to her hotel room to read a book, and the two partners went to the plaza to sit and watch the people stroll by. Four Mexicans in brightly colored clothes gathered with stringed musical instruments and a cornet. A small crowd surrounded them as they played. Lighthorse and Sammy enjoyed the music, too.

Then Sammy said, "It's been some day. I reckon I'll hit the blankets before anything else happens."

"Me, too. I've lived through enough happenings to keep me going awhile."

Walking across the plaza, Sammy chuckled, "I was thinking, if we told anybody about everything that's happened, they wouldn't believe it."

"I don't think I'll tell anybody."

"Me either. Not until I'm sixty."

At the breakfast table the next morning, after they'd cleaned their platters and drained their coffee cups, the woman turned serious gray eyes on Lighthorse. "Lighthorse, can I talk to Sammy alone for a few minutes?"

The Indian looked from one to the other and said, "Sure. I'll be outside." He pushed his chair back, stood and left.

"Sammy." She put her hand on top of his. It was a warm, soft hand, and it sent a tingle all through Sammy. He could feel himself blushing. "Why don't you go to St. Louis with me?" The gray eyes were locked onto his. "I don't like traveling alone, I don't like dining at a table for one, and . . ." She paused a second. "I don't like sleeping alone."

When the implication of what she'd said sunk in, Sammy's heartbeat quickened. Exhilarating thoughts stirred inside him. Sleep with her? He remembered how beautiful and exciting she'd looked naked in the moonlight. She was every man's dream of a woman, and she wanted to sleep with him. He could have her and spending money and a fun town like St. Louis. What more could a man ask for?

She talked on. "St. Louis is a wonderful city. There are stage plays, operas, and the finest restaurants anywhere. I love that European cuisine. There are stores that sell the finest clothing money can buy. I'll buy beautiful gowns, and you'll be handsome in a dinner jacket with a bow tie. Oh, we'll have a wonderful time."

And just as suddenly as his heart had climbed into his throat, it dropped into his stomach.

She squeezed his hand. "You have no other plans. Please say you'll do it."

"Well, uh . . ." How to say it?

"Is something the matter?"

He had to clear his throat and start over. "Well, uh, you see, uh, you're a beautiful woman, Mrs. Wilcox. Any man you choose would be a very lucky man. But . . . you know, uh, you're fine silky gowns, and I'm Levi's and a flannel shirt and boots. You're opera; I'm a fiddle and a gittar. You're European cuisine; I'm beefsteak and Mexican beans." Turning tortured eyes toward her, he begged for understanding.

Her gaze dropped to her hand on top of his. Slowly, she removed her hand. "I'm disappointed, Sammy. I'm very disappointed. But I do understand." She forced a smile. "After all, a lady can't have everything."

They walked her to the stage stop, carrying her satchel and a new leather suitcase. The coach was ready, with four passengers and the U.S. mail inside. Four horses were chomping on their snaffle bits and shuffling their feet. The teamster climbed up to his high seat beside a gent with a double-barreled shotgun and gathered the driving lines. Looking down on the woman and two men, he said, "All aboard."

Blinking moist eyes, Mrs. Wilcox said, "I'll never forget you fellas. You're perfect gentlemen, both of you."

She climbed into the coach and took a backward-facing seat. The teamster hollered, "Heeyup," the four horses lunged into their collars, and she was gone.

The partners watched the coach until it was out of sight, not speaking. Finally, Lighthorse said, "It's a long ride to Fort Union. I'd better get started."

Sammy stood with his thumbs hooked inside his belt as Lighthorse saddled his bay horse and tied his saddlebags and blanket roll behind the cantle.

"Write me a letter when you get to wherever you go. You know where I'll be."

"I'll do that." Shaking his head, Sammy added, "You're gonna be wearing a trail to Fort Bayard and back."

"Yeah"—Lighthorse grinned—"but I'm sure gonna enjoy the ride back."

They shook hands. No hugs, no back slapping. Just shook. Then Lighthorse, too, was gone.

Sammy wasted no time feeling lonely. He walked back to the plaza, across it and down a side street. He paused a moment at the door to the Sandia Saddlery, then went inside.

An elderly man with a round, wrinkled, pleasant face looked at him over the top of half-lens glasses, looked and listened.

"Wal, I sorta had in mind a younger feller, some kid in his teen years."

"I'm not too old to learn, and I'm used to hard work and long days."

Faded blue eyes went over Sammy, inch by inch. "I can't pay you much."

"I was in the army a long time and I've saved some money. I don't need much. Just let me learn the trade."

"Got a place to stay?"

"I'll find a place."

"When can you start?"

"Right now."

"Wal, you better find a place to stay—there's a coupla purty good boardin'houses in town—then come back in the mornin' ready to go to work. Say seven-thirty."

"Yes sir." Sammy held out his hand to shake. They shook.

As he walked to the Casa Grande Hotel, from where he would begin his search for a new home, Sammy felt good. He felt good about Mrs. Wilcox; he felt good about Lighthorse.

And he felt good about himself.

THE BLOOD BOND SERIES

by William W. Johnstone

The continuing adventures of blood brothers, Matt Bodine and Sam Two Wolves — two of the fastest guns in the west.

BLOOD BOND   (2724, $3.95)

BLOOD BOND #2:
BROTHERHOOD OF THE GUN   (3044, $3.95)

BLOOD BOND #3:
GUNSIGHT CROSSING   (3473, $3.95)

BLOOD BOND #4:
GUNSMOKE AND GOLD   (3664, $3.50)

BLOOD BOND #5:
DEVIL CREEK CROSSFIRE   (3799, $3.50)

BLOOD BOND #6:
SHOOTOUT AT GOLD CREEK   (4222, $3.50)

BLOOD BOND #7:
SAN ANGELO SHOOTOUT   (4466, $3.99)

Available wherever paperbacks are sold, or order direct from the Publisher. Send cover price plus 50¢ per copy for mailing and handling to Penguin USA, P.O. Box 999, c/o Dept. 17109, Bergenfield, NJ 07621. Residents of New York and Tennessee must include sales tax. DO NOT SEND CASH.